The Antiquarian

The Antiquarian

Gustavo Faverón Patriau

Translated from the Spanish
by Joseph Mulligan

Black Cat
an imprint of Grove/Atlantic
New York

FIRST EDITION

This novel is entirely a work of fiction. The names, characters, and incidents
portrayed in it are the work of the author's imagination. Any resemblance to actual
persons, living or dead, events, or localities is entirely coincidental.

First published in Spanish in 2010 as *El Anticuario* by Ediciones Peisa (Peru).

Published simultaneously in Canada
Printed in the United States of America

ISBN: 978-0-8021-2160-8
eBook ISBN: 978-0-8021-9285-1

Black Cat
an imprint of Grove/Atlantic, Inc.
154 West 14th Street
New York, NY 10011

Distributed by Publishers Group West

www.groveatlantic.com

14 15 16 17   10 9 8 7 6 5 4 3 2 1

For Carolyn, as always

Every time you name yourself,
you name someone else.

Bertolt Brecht

How can I speak of love, of your Kingdom's tender hills,
when I live like a cat on a pole surrounded by water?
How can I call the hair, hair
the tooth, tooth
the tail, tail
and not ever name the rat?

Antonio Cisneros, "Oración"

The Antiquarian

PROLOGUE

According to Conrad Lycosthenes' wife, who was a foreigner, the women of her country used to lay eggs like hens. Conrad killed her and on her deathbed found a yellow egg and through a crack in the shell saw a sleeping face that was identical to his own. Ramihrdus of Cambrai was born of a virgin hen and they killed him: 1076. Gherardo Segarelli preached to the wise men in the barn and they killed him: 1300. Fra Dolcino bred chickens and roosters and they killed him: 1307. This is what I hear: Jan Hus made Peter crow thrice and they killed him: 1415. Jacob Hutter disemboweled his disciples and they killed him: 1536. Anne Askew quenched the thirst of her chicks with her own blood and they killed her: 1546.

This is what I've been hearing for an indeterminable period of time. I open and close my eyes and then I open them again. I don't know if minutes, hours, or weeks have gone by. In the penumbra, as in the light, I hear the same list unraveling: Nicholas Ridley's feathers were plucked for being the king of the Jews and they killed him: 1555. Gioffredo Varaglia bought thirty hens from Judas and they killed him: 1558. Bernardino Conte named his first child Magdalene and they killed him: 1560. From time to time, a gruff, stammering voice cuts in and out, and I open my eyes to see the room I am in. On certain occasions I notice that night has fallen, or perhaps that dawn has already come. I then reach the realization that I am in a hospital. And I listen: Diego López founded his church with the effigy of a sparrow-hawk carved in stone and they killed him: 1583. I fall asleep, and in my dreams I recognize that I am in *another* hospital, one that's larger and ever bustling. And I recognize that it's my own voice that I'm hearing. My face is bandaged: the strips of gauze press against my nose, ears, and eyes. That's why it's hard to look at objects. But nevertheless I look. And when my gaze ventures beyond the bandages, the gauze feels like a half-decayed peel that separates the outer world from the inner, distinguishing reality from dream from memory. In these early moments I don't know which is which. Nor do I know (as of now) how long I have been lying in this bed and why I am here in this hospital. Days go by and objects gain clarity: there are doctors and nurses who tend to me, although no one comes in to visit me—my wife died years ago. Was it in this hospital or was it in another? I don't know. I do know that Giordano Bruno invented a system to remember everything using only the feathers on one wing and they killed him: 1600. Bartolomeo Coppino wrapped a crown of thorns around his crest and they killed him: 1601.

Of the doctors who come to see me, one always seems to be smiling and the other shows no expression whatsoever on his face, like he's wearing a porcelain mask. Days ago I asked him to bring me a pen and paper, and he in turn tasked a nurse to provide me with notebooks and pencils, and after spending three days scribbling, this morning I finally decided to write. Bartholomew Legate censored the plebeians' squawks and they killed him: 1612. I write down this first line: *It is an ancient story, which for others commenced centuries ago, and for me, at least fifteen or twenty years back.* Then I cross out that phrase and write a different one—*Three years had gone by since the night when Daniel killed Juliana, and on the telephone his voice sounded like someone else's*—because I don't want to begin my story by way of hyperbole. I don't wish to tell what happened centuries ago. If at times I revert to the prehistory of my story, it is for the sole purpose of gaining precision. Suffice it to say that one morning, four weeks ago (now I am certain), I awoke calmly, routinely, not in this bed, but in the one in my house, as is to be expected, and I was pouring myself a cup of coffee when the telephone rang.

ONE

Three years had gone by since the night when Daniel killed Juliana, and on the telephone his voice sounded like someone else's. As if nothing had happened, he called to invite me to lunch. As if lunch with him still meant going to a casually chosen restaurant or to his parents' house, where we used to hang out, surrounded by shelves packed with books, manuscripts, notepads, and bundles of papers folded into quarters, and corbels stuffed with thousands of volumes with amber spines, cracked leather covers, and glistening dust jackets. As if visiting him still meant, like it did before, ascending that wrought iron spiral staircase toward the library-bedroom in which Daniel used to spend every waking hour of the day, day upon day, week after week, deciphering marginalia in tomes that no one reads anymore, having breakfast and lunch in his pajamas, putting his feet up on the desk, with a magnifying glass in his left hand and an expression of astonishment rippling across his face. Back then, it did not mean entering that awful place where they had interned him, or rather, where he had interned himself in order to escape an even more confining prison.

Daniel had been my closest friend since our early college days. We were inseparable during those now distant years, when our vocations were being decided and with them, our lives. I chose psychology, thereafter psycholinguistics, and barely had I left the department when I married an irresistible, elegant colleague who fell terminally ill and died two years later, leaving me alone in a

4

house I no longer recognized, with a collection of letters from lovers who had given her more affection than I had—and afterward I no longer had the strength to build another relationship that would not decline into brevity and anonymity. Daniel, abstaining from juvenile engagements, was almost immediately seized by the study of history, books, and antiquities. He delved into a world of frantic and febrile readers who would consume tortuous volumes with the voracity of multi-cephalic beasts that spent their existence submerged in archives and hundred-year-old catalogues, or in meetings of bibliophile relic-traffickers, scholars who would purchase entire libraries from the widows of their dearest friends, paying derisory sums, in perpetual search for the coveted uncut tome that, once acquired, they could deflower with a pair of shears or with a blade in the obscurity of some dim den.

Daniel was younger than all of them—they were old enough to be his parents or grandparents—but for some reason they treated him as if he were an old Sherpa on some wilderness expedition into which they had accidentally, unfortunately or perhaps cunningly ventured while hiding certain objectives that none of them dared confess. One of them was Gálvez, a retired pettifogger who, then and for many years now, has divided his time between practicing ornithology and hunting incunabula and ecclesiastic archives, a solitary and despotic soul who obeyed only his own intuitions, Daniel's silent admonitions, or the whims of his old maid of a daughter, his sole companion at home. Another of them, Mireaux, was the hunchbacked proprietor of a conservative tabloid— aristocratic in appearance, abounding with arithmetical phrases and intransigence, he as much as his paper—and this man possessed a high-pitched voice that seemed to squeak out of his nose or escape through the folds of corrugated skin that covered his throat. The third, Pastor, was an ex–nautical captain, older than

Daniel but younger than the others, who had retired from the Navy years ago in order to dodge his transfer to the Red Zone— a destination that officers back then, though really not that long ago, understood as a deadly curse, if not a sentence to perpetual horror. Pastor moved in semicircles when he walked and, with his outstretched fingers, drew spherical flowering figures in the air as he spoke—that is, when he produced the whine of that dark and undulating voice of his, like the squirting of squid ink, which he proffered each time he wished to lay to rest his discrepancy with other people over a topic that had become the center of a dispute.

I never knew them very well, but my relationship with Daniel increased the frequency of our encounters. We shared a superficial friendship of short conversations and banal references, except for Mireaux, with whom my dealings were greater, because one of his nieces, who was aphasic and autistic, had been my patient for many years. The four of them—Daniel and Mireaux at first, and then Pastor and Gálvez—casually to start and then quite often visited the only bookstore of antiquities in the city they felt was deserving of their respect. They soon became regulars and, metonymically or maybe by metastasis, as Daniel joked, ended up shareholders, and then expanded the store, transforming it into an emporium of printed relics, engravings, charcoal drawings, nineteenth-century oil paintings, documents from the colonial era, the emancipation, the First Republic, which they acquired and sold or, so say certain unminded tongues, stealthily purloined from the humblest of provincial churches and decapitated chapels in the middle of nowhere, or which they purchased from needy debtors who were ignorant to the fact that between the papers and books of a recently deceased uncle, father, or grandfather was an unmistakable edition of such and such a volume from such and such a collection, which Daniel or Pastor or Gálvez or Mireaux, or perhaps all of them, had sought for years on end. Together, the four men became the principal proprietors of that bookstore, little by little emasculating the influence of the original owner, before ousting him once and for all. So it was that each proprietor added to the old catalogue what he was willing to volunteer from his private collection, and by the end of this operation, the four of them christened the new bookstore with the curious and amusing name by which they had come to call themselves: The Circle.

I was often tempted to enter that community of unforgivable bibliopaths, but I never did. I am, as I was then, a practical reader, dazzled only on occasion by Daniel's findings and his passion. I always stayed close to him throughout the end of our boyhood and over the nearly two decades that he would spend building that legendary library that book dealers, intellectuals, and university professors spoke of with reverence and envy, in the way that initiates of a sect speak of the sanctuary inhabited by their mystical leader. Indeed, we had stayed close until the morning when I learned, not from him, but from the headlines of several newspapers at a newsstand downtown—this being three years ago—that Daniel had killed Juliana, his fiancée, stabbing her thirty-six times, supposedly in a fit of jealousy. He had tried to burn her body, then stuck her in the trunk of his car and left her there for hours. Then he had driven from the beach to the city, returning to his parents' house, where they still lived, with the slashed cadaver in the trunk. He had tried to take his own life with a gunshot to the head, but was unsuccessful. Chance, it turns out, had decided that this very gun, stolen from the dresser at the house, should jam and thereby give his father time to rush toward his son and save his life with a clout to the back of his head.

I did not see him during the days that ensued. Defeated by a feeling of absurd and unjustifiable guilt, I did not dare attend the trial or visit him in prison; I did not speak with his parents or with his brother; never did I go near the psychiatric ward, a mere five blocks from my apartment, where the judge had ordered that he be interned, ruling him insane and keeping him out of prison in exchange for a secret payment which, nonetheless, half of the city gossiped about with the same certainty as they did theories about the motives of the crime: adultery, exploitation, an intricate incident between traffickers of archeological remains. Lies. And I had not heard his voice again until he asked me to have lunch with him that afternoon, and I, without enough time to come up with an excuse, said sure, I would be right over. At that moment it was impossible to imagine that my conversation with Daniel would be plagued with riddles and silences that would require me, for the purpose of quelling them, to transform into a detective from dusk to dawn and hit the streets to capture certain specters, delve deep into the well of a distant memory, and pursue, through the labyrinthine minds of loons, the fickle face of two or three ghosts. Edward Wightman crumbled the body of Christ to distribute it amongst the birds and they killed him: 1612. Gabriel Malagrida drove out the merchants from the coop and they killed him: 1761.

TWO

The trees that lined the avenue swayed to the rhythm of the wind, their limbs hanging over cars and pedestrians like the outstretched arms of beggars. At the hospital entrance, a blind girl with bony hands, wearing a pink skirt, was selling candy and soda, while an elderly woman a few yards away was pressing her ear against the telephone booth, as if trying to overhear a secret message. When I walked through the door, the sound of the cars and the birds filtered through the front hall in a veil of granular light that made the people inside look like transparent objects: projections rising from the ground up that became blurrier the higher they rose, such that a cloud of translucent bodies formed at the height of my eyes. The echo of my footsteps bounced off the walls, throughout the hallway, where family members of live-in patients sat in small seats alongside those who came for appointments. Upon the reception desk at this end of the hall—a desk with rusted edges, covered with calendars, business card holders, and laminated folders—a pile of notebooks hid the wan face of a nurse who repeated my name several times before sliding my ID into a little flesh-colored wooden box and pointing out the way to Daniel's room.

As I walked through the third door, which squeaked closed on a hinged metal arm, I heard labored snoring, then a shriek and a series of cackles or coughs that, for some reason, I perceived as just a few of the many others that fell into some soft silence. I had been there before, a while ago. I remembered the following hallway like a high, cavernous, and endless black hole, but I saw that it was, rather, a tunnel of opaque light, a low ceiling, and an unfinished cement floor, which repeatedly turned to the left. Its straight stretches became shorter and shorter, and its turns each sharper than the last, in such a way that, if my memory does not fail me in this too, the hallway would close in on itself, like the coiling of a serpent, until reaching the great doorway that opened up to the courtyard of gravel and sand: the center of the ward. All the doors were on the left-hand side. They were white or gray or of distinct facades, as if each one came from a different time period. I attentively scanned them, looking for number sixteen. For a considerable lapse of time I had not seen anyone, but next to door fifteen there was someone, difficult to say if it was a woman or man. This was an obscure little figure, crouching down, wrapped in a poncho woven with dirty threads, whose astonished eyes, fixed on a point above the threshold of the door, gave me the impression that they had discovered up there, floating beneath the ceiling, a crystal ball or a map that held the key to the future. When I passed by this person, it turned its face toward me, adopting an uncomfortable stance, and it said, "Here even light lives on." It was the voice of a woman.

I kept walking and again, she repeated, "Here even light lives on." She then added the following words with emphasis, as if each were the cipher of some greater, secret word: "Glamorous, opulent, ornate doors before your eyes," she said. I turned to the left two more times before reaching number sixteen. A layer of yellowish dust soiled the half-opened door, and an aroma of phosphorus and kerosene lingered in the air. I knocked softly and the wooden door swung inward, bringing into view, on the floor, in the center of the room, a skinny man, dressed in black, who was squatting, gazing at the pilot light of a stove, while holding a recently blown-out match in his hand. He waved hello. With eyes small and familiar and the large, maroon, cruciform burn on his forehead, he arched his brows as if to say "Yes, I recognize you, Gustavo, I haven't forgotten you," and then with his chin he pointed to the only chair and sat down cross-legged, with his arms stretched out. "I've become a cook," he said. "Lunch is on me."

I sat in the chair, and he stayed on the floor below, facing me, fixing his eyes on the burner. The room—with its greenish walls, a narrow bed, a night table, and a bookshelf devoid of even one book—did not have any windows or mirrors. In the corner opposite the door a small oil lamp radiated cloudy light which shimmered through the stained-glass panes, projecting vague silhouettes on the wall. "I apologize for not coming sooner," I said, and it was my intention to add to this another thought but it refused to come all the way to my lips. (Juliana's face, on the other hand, was stirred up in my memory, superimposed onto the spirals of smoke from the little lamp: her black eyes, with parallel wrinkles of crow's feet; her upper lip, slim and quivering, which seemed to nap upon its lower, soft, colorless counterpart.) Daniel opened a box, emptied the contents into a pan on the stove, and the aroma of fried food mingled with the other smells. "There are no electrical outlets in this room," he said. "They put covers on the sockets one day, without explaining why." He smiled, and his face resembled the face I remembered. He then added, "I don't believe it's to keep me from taking my own life. Who kills himself by sticking a fork into an electrical socket anyway?" And his laughter sounded like a squawk.

That afternoon we ate lunch in silence, barely exchanging a word. There was a single plastic knife that, in Daniel's hands, bent and produced a tenuous screech on the plate, and when he slid it toward me from time to time, I would use it, the remnants of meat from his plate mixing in with those on mine. "Something has happened," he said abruptly. He stacked the empty plates on each other and placed the plastic silverware and the two paper cups on top of them. "I need you to help me—that's why I called." He rose from the floor, extending his legs like an expanding accordion, and then asked, "Do you want to see the courtyard?" He walked toward the door in a hurry, stamping his feet and swinging his arms, as if he had just learned to walk and was trying to do so without making a mistake. He left the room and I followed him into the hallway, quickening my pace to keep up with him. "There are forty of us in this ward," he said, "and there's another ward too, identical to this one, but separated. Two wards, two courtyards, two hallways." And then he squawked out another laugh. "I should be in the other, the one with the violent patients, but my mother has given a ton of money to the hospital, I don't know how much, so that they let me live here."

We took another left turn, and then another, and at the end of the second turn we reached the shortest stretch of the hallway. On one side of the courtyard, there was a man in a faded suit, a doctor perhaps, with an unlit cigarette between his lips. What little sunlight was left in the day grazed the back of his neck. The man flashed a glance at me and then eyed Daniel, and after a moment muttered, "Easy, take it easy." My friend headed in the direction of the bathroom, saying, "Just a second, I'll be right back." Once we were left alone, the man with the cigarette asked me if I had any matches. I reflexively checked my pockets before telling him that it had been years since I quit smoking, and he retorted an unintelligible reply. On one side of the courtyard four women were sitting in a semicircle with a nurse who kept asking them trivialities and overemphasized her gestures of emotion or interest. At the other end, a young man and an elderly fellow, standing side by side, were absorbed in their observation of the trunk of a leafless, scraggly bush. The man with the cigarette attentively stared at a folded newspaper he held in his grimy hand. On the edge of the page there was a series of numbers jotted in pencil. "So you've come to visit Daniel, have you?" he said, without raising his eyes from the page.

"That's right," I said.

"Good," the man said. "People here need that. No matter how many visitors they have, they're still alone inside, but it never hurts to have contact with the outside world."

I listened to him with difficulty. His voice was gruff and remote. His words departed from a hindered mouth, as if some words clouded others over. "Throughout the years," said the man, "I've seen many people exile themselves in that inner loneliness, only in the end to lose their remaining sanity to nostalgia and the melancholy of confinement. This place can kill anyone. And I'm not merely referring to the patients. A psychiatric ward bears the greatest likeness to Hell itself than any other of man's earthly constructions, with circles and cells for the terminally ill. It's a cloister duplicated for those who, upon arrival, are already imprisoned in themselves." His voice barely found its way past his lips, which remained pressed together, one against the other, holding the unlit cigarette in place. I told him that at least it was better to be here inside than to walk around like one of those wandering madmen who can be seen all over the city. "I suppose it is," he said, "although at times I get the sense that, on the outside, exposed to reality, they have their last chance to confront it, to be recognized by it, even if they don't manage to see it as it is."

"Do you really believe that?" I asked.

He didn't utter a word but nodded his head and immediately stretched out his arm to slowly unfold the newspaper he was gripping with his fingertips. "The thing is," he said, "I think these people deserve the chance to circulate through the world, if for nothing else than to destroy it in the end. Here, all the aspects of their behavior that doctors and nurses judge abnormal are instantly repressed. They slowly disappear, even though the instinct that gave rise to them is not vanquished. Madness is forever, but it gets penned up, confined to the deepest recesses of their mind, behind every gesture of pain and unrest. Do you know what it's like to have the specter of illness inside you and be forbidden to express its symptoms, in such a way that you never learn to live in intimacy?" I gave no response. It seemed to me the question was not directed at anyone in particular.

He thumbed through the pages of the newspaper with purposeful rapidity, until he found what he was searching for. "Look here," he said. "They discovered this recently in San Francisco. Two months ago, an illusionist confined himself in a Plexiglas box, six feet in width, six feet in height, and three feet at the base. He had them suspend it, hooked to a steel cable, from the Golden Gate Bridge, over the Pacific Ocean, not far from Alcatraz. He had vowed to remain enclosed for forty-four days, without eating any solid food, only drinking water and receiving an I.V. for the next six weeks. He succeeded. They extracted him from the box at the end of six weeks: he was tumefactive and nearly insane, his fingers purple, his eyes dead, his skin scorched and sticking to his spine, deranged and so removed from this world that only on the third or fourth day, in a hospital, was he able to comprehend that he had lived up to his word. All of this, of course, appeared in the newspapers, and perhaps you've seen him on television. But what has been discovered just this week adds a mind-boggling twist to the story. Across from the bridge, upon the bay's western slope, there is a neighborhood by the name of Presidio. It's an old military burg, a maze of winding woods and identical redbrick buildings, long converted into a residential zone. In one of those buildings, whipped by the frigid winds coming off the water, a man divided the space into minuscule apartments, each with its own bathroom, and he tends to rent them to university students or undocumented immigrants. So, putting three months' rent down in advance, a woman took an apartment in that building with a view of the bridge from which the illusionist's box was going to hang. The landlord never did get to know her, and three months later tried to contact her on the telephone, but no luck. Days later, he found the keys to the apartment in the mailbox and understood this as a sign that the renter had already moved out. One morning, he went to the apartment with the intention of cleaning it so that he could rent it out again. On the ground, next to the window, curled up with a blanket over her back and a pair of binoculars clenched in her hand—a notebook and two or three pens atop a stool—he discovered the cadaver of an elderly woman: a frail, gaunt body without any muscles, her skin translucent and her ears scored by a network of violet filaments, her veins now filled with putrid blood. The stench, obviously, gave away her decomposition. But perhaps you have already guessed that she was not really an elderly woman. She was the woman who had rented his place for the last three months. The matter came under official investigation. In the notebook, the detectives found the answers to a good part of their questions: The woman had subjected herself to the same test as the illusionist, beginning at the same time, and had even surpassed him. She'd refrained from eating for forty-six days, and had scrupulously recorded on those pages the sensations of her experiment: the dizziness and extreme weakness, the iridescence of her skin, the frenetic rhythm of her heart with each movement, the chronic asphyxia in the final afternoons, the consumption of her tongue with eruptions of boils and scars, the unusual sound of her joints contracting and expanding, the trembling of her forehead and temples, the bruising of her arms and legs, the periodic creaking of her spinal cord. Everything. She also left instructions for how her journal of agony should be published. Now, you tell me, was that woman mad? I bet you'll say she was. And I'd probably agree. Does that mean she should've realized that she was mad earlier, or that someone else, once having identified her madness, should've locked her up in an asylum to prevent her from consummating that insane finale?"

This time, the man fixed his eyes on me and awaited my response. "I imagine," I said, "if the behavior of that woman had implied an end of that nature, then it would not have been absurd to try to protect her from herself." And he replied, "That's right: that's how we think about madness, like a danger of annihilation, the risk of an attack capable of destroying someone, either the patient or anyone else who happens to be in his or her vicinity. Out of all the illnesses in history that were thought to be contagious and are now confirmed not to be, madness and leprosy are the only ones we continue to see as an epidemic risk, as if living amongst the mad, speaking to them, being around them, could somehow drive the observer mad." The man folded the newspaper and placed it under his arm. Behind us, the semicircle of patients had dissolved and in its place a little old man with a defenseless face was kneeling with a blank notebook in front of his eyes. "Madness is only contagious in a place like this," said the man. "On the street, docile madmen are hard to come by, and furious or repulsive crazies are a dime a dozen. But, in here, all together, they're an irresistible force, like inertia and gravity, capable of attracting and consuming everything. Whoever comes here with an illness indiscriminately acquires them all. Visiting Daniel will help. Before there's nothing left in him of the person he once was."

At that moment Daniel arrived from the bathroom, drying his hands on his pants. The man with the cigarette took out a pen to write another number in the margins of the newspaper, substituting a grin for the word *goodbye*. The courtyard was an uncovered quadrilateral, with two bald bushes and benches on each side, on one of which a woman sat slowly eating a piece of bread. "That's all she eats," said Daniel, "only bread. It sometimes seems as though it were the same slice of bread every day."

"Here?" I asked, pointing in the direction of the benches with my outstretched arm. He waited for me to take a seat and dropped down again, this time onto the ground of gravel and sand. "That doctor," I said, "seems like a good guy, doesn't he? But he gives me the impression that he's going through some sort of vocational crisis."

"He's not a doctor," Daniel said, "at least not in the sense that you mean. He was one of the psychiatrists in this ward for many years, but one day, or so they say, he quit his job and the following week showed up, this time to stay, with a suitcase full of clothes and a box of books. He's been a patient of the hospital for six, seven years now. He was already here when I arrived. And even then, he was harping on the same topic that I'm sure he was talking to you about just now. He speaks of nothing else. What's most unsettling about a madman is his sane conversation, isn't that how it goes? This place is full of people like him. As you know, mental illnesses make you speak, but they usually transform language into ritual. Come on, let's get down to business. I'm going to tell you a bunch of stories today," he said, taking me by the arm as he let out another squawk.

The Antiquarian reads: A very young woman, almost a girl, escapes from her house to the skirt of the mountain, her child strapped to her back, tied tight around her shoulders by a multicolored cloth. The jealous spirit of her husband follows them into the countryside. A party of masked men whiffs the air behind her, follows her scent, and surrounds her at the entrance to an abandoned village. The screams of the woman fade into the jubilation of the men. She, face up, her eyes two black dots, united (as by a wire) on the highest branch of a ficus tree, her back pressing onto the edge of a stone: the poor woman, almost a girl, lying upon an altar, an unending line of strangers entering and exiting her body. The last man, unable to penetrate her, pulls out a knife from his pocket and cuts the palm of the girl's hand. He marks her, drawing a single winding and curvy character, like the beak of a gull, and in the morning, she is someone else, her name is different, or she is now nameless, her daughter is nowhere to be found, and it is hard for her to tell if she ever even had a daughter or just dreamed that she did, and she sets out across gray and yellow valleys and hills, entering villages of country folk who watch her walk by with suspicion, and she asks everyone about her lost daughter, she explains what her daughter is like, or should be like, until, in a one-horse town, someone tells her, I know where she could be, and this personage leads her to a lost meadow behind a hill of weeds to a black stream, and he says to her, Might she be one of these? and the woman, almost a girl, looks into the bottom of the stream and sees a row of identical children, eyes open, mouths open, hands reaching toward the sky. The Antiquarian closes his book and pauses for a moment.

THREE

"Do you know where *La Verdad* is?"

"Of course I do. It's right in the center of everything."

"How much to go there?"

"Six."

I met Daniel during my first semester at the university, a long time ago. He was a skinny, awkward young man, who roamed through the walkways, courtyards, and classrooms with a flushed face, wandering eyes, and a hollow expression that seemed to anticipate the years that awaited him. Our classmates, incapable of mustering more than gestures of indolence and gazes of secret indifference, interpreted his attitude as a sign of disdain and smugness. Time taught me that such absentmindedness, the way in which he appeared to suddenly slip from the present moment and silently transport himself into environs and epochs that no one else could access, was neither the expression of arrogance nor, as I once suspected, the involuntary mask of timidity. It was something else: Daniel embraced his awareness of being different and also his displeasure at being so, as if he were clinging to the sole life preserver capable of keeping him afloat before an imminent shipwreck. Securing his self-preservation, which he did on a daily basis, Daniel hardly tried to veil his knowledge with the ignorance—foreign to him, imperceptible to me—of those who surrounded him. In class, he intervened only when it was obvious that no one, neither students nor professors, would endeavor to explain a phenomenon, intuit the root of a problem, or supply a debate with some indispensable argument in order to lead it away from the danger of mediocrity. But he did this in such a way that his scandalous erudition reinforced the walls of that solitary fortress in which Daniel hid other stigmas of his difference.

For that reason, and since my thoughts were then and still are now, nearly twenty years later, meager in comparison with Daniel's intellectual splendors, it is not easy to explain why he chose me out of everyone to be his friend—why he gave me permission to enter that fortressed tower which had become his life. At a certain moment he decided to sit next to me in class; then he began to modulate the timing of his arrivals and departures so that he would meet me at the classroom door, in line at the cafeteria, during breaks in that earthen-colored rotunda that was like a recently excavated ruin (the naval of a miniature world where we students of the Literature Department took up residence around a stunted and battered tree, so similar to the center square of some provincial township). Over time, he began to lend me his books and decided to explain them to me, to summarize or to expand on them, proposing prodigious or ridiculous exegeses, extravagant interpretations in a most unusual argot. Whether out of wisdom or lunacy, Daniel excitedly expounded these ideas in parks and on sidewalks like a flimsy orchestra director whose arms would trace elliptical shapes and tremble when upraised, improvising interpretations that extrapolated a psychoanalysis manual as if it were the plot of a love story, and he transformed it into a hagiography, a history of law, a teleological argument, or, perhaps (and this was his predilection), the core thread of a treatise on the art of war. And then Daniel would smile as he reached some untenable conclusion, and would look into the eyes of any stranger who happened to be nearby as if seeking confirmation of his syllogisms;

or else he would simply jump to another topic until slowly but surely he returned to his state of exaltation, whereupon the entire process would begin anew.

In those early years, our friendship took place on two main stages that quickly multiplied into four. The first two were the campus and the long avenue that began at its front gate, a wide wasteland, colorless but teeming with violent aromas and advertisements written with bright letters and suspect orthography that announced daily specials at restaurants and upcoming events, discounted appliances and wicker furniture, personal services and transportation, all along sidewalks and intersections that unfolded in blind procession, squeezed toward an imaginary downtown. Seen from street level, the avenue appeared unending and straight; from above it must have looked like a long strip of tape curled in a spiral. Together for much of the time, we stomped through that mutating street five times per week in order to arrive at our classes, and little by little we each accepted the risk of straying into the side streets, venturing around unknown corners as if they were portals into the world of the Other. At my insistence, Daniel acquired the custom of taking to a certain winding and dim alley, lined with houses stacked on top of each other, which led directly to a neighborhood of somber bordellos, cantinas, and smoking dens, with green walls on the outside and small red salons and private rooms within.

One of these was a dismal establishment, with small tables bunched together and white plastic chairs, that served strange liquors which seemed to change color when left to their lonesome for too long, and this became our hideout for many an afternoon. It had no official name. The drunkards there, who did not appear to be patrons but rather objects of a decorative nature, called it Japonesita's Palace, in honor of a matron with a southern accent, sagging breasts, and slits for eyes. She rarely was present, yet still supervised everything from a portrait that hung two feet from the door. At Japonesita's Palace, Daniel and I were indubitably the most conspicuous persons. We spent many hours incapacitated by the creeping effects of those infernal libations, and the second round would motivate us to open our backpacks and begin to recite the culminating passages of whichever book we had on hand. Initially, the hookers were fearful of us, a couple of snot-nosed kids who never knew what to say unless we found it written on a page; but later they warmed up, and every once in a while demanded that we repeat some fragment that they judged to be memorable. Only once out of some five hundred times did one of us accept the vaudevillian adulation from one of those plump and rotund women who stirred throughout the establishment at every hour, whose nicknames evoked jungles or deserts or mysteries of sexual acrobatics: The Jaguar, The Sultana, The Centipede. So it was that one or the other of us would grab ahold of one of those hands with its cracked and painted fingernails and ascend that rickety stairway so narrow that it seemed to be painted on the wall, until we reached a room with a wooden floor and a single window with little curtains of worn canvas and a picture of Jesus presiding over a bed with satin sheets. There we would make love to The Jaguar as if we were on a hunt, to The Sultana as if we were being watched by a eunuch, or to The Centipede lost in the garden of her restless extremities, and then immediately come back downstairs, without even completely washing up, to continue the conversation that had been put on hold by dint of an impulse that at first was inexplicable and afterward seemed empty and purposeless. "Those boys need a road map to find a crotch," one of them said, whichever one she was, but we were already on to something else.

More often than not, Daniel forced me to forfeit these clandestine jaunts and took me to his house, to his library-bedroom, where he obliged me to plunge into that opaque atmosphere made of particles of paper, molecules of books, that leapt into the air each time we opened an ancient volume, flipped a shiny page that was stiff as cartilage, or precipitately closed the cover of some small rectangle of paper and leather. It was in his house that I discovered that books were merely one of the many manifestations of Daniel's need to cloister himself in worlds separated from reality or in parallel realities. Film and painting, of course, were also clearly refuges, but, despite their fantastic pleasure, Daniel harbored a special weakness for what he called the "architecture of dreams," which was not one of those psychological categories that he had chided with such complacence on hurried walks across campus, but rather the sardonic name he used to describe his passion for constructing houses and buildings out of paper, Sheetrock, or balsa wood. To call them houses, however, does not do them justice. They were scale models of palaces, mansions, fortresses, and museums, replicas of observatories, estates, and lighthouses, which Daniel, with the help of Sofía—his scrawny, whiny little sister, nine or ten years of age—would construct and display on desktops, tables, pedestals, or makeshift altars of flat-topped pyramids of books stacked up in the corner of his room. Sofía was a caring but strange girl, and rather evasive, for she always went about dressed in attire that conveniently disguised her latest mischief, and she spoke in a squealing and sonorous tiny voice, improvising choruses and carols or enthusiastically engaging in conversations with invisible people. On the other hand, she never spoke to anyone who was of flesh and bone, nor did she seem concerned about obtaining any response, to such an extent that, quite often, she selected the words she knew and added new ones of an imaginary language, to which the adults in her surroundings responded at times with monosyllabic grunts in a show of solidarity. She would come down from on high to speak normally only when it became necessary to negotiate with her brother the finer points of the latest model that the two of them had set out to construct. And so it was that, from the hands of those two architects and masons, masters of origami and model-making, there came forth delicate prototypes of castles, mosques, and citadels with cellophane windows, cretonne curtains, and tinplate doors. However, if Sofía adopted mere mortal language, it was with the warning that her good temperament was in recess. From then on, she was the boss. Her soprano bawling and impossible contortions of a neonate diva became a calamity for Daniel, who transformed from older brother to disgruntled servant, with the sole intention of doing things exactly as the girl decreed. And Sofía did not moderate her laughable exigency until the end, when the construction had been finished and there arose in the middle of the library-bedroom a tiny Château Mont-Royal, a miniature Alhambra, a minuscule Chichén Itzá.

With bursts of joy from a baseline of cantankerousness, Sofía was a sickly girl. A congenital disease debilitated her bones and muscles, making her prone to sudden fractures and tears, not always caused by any apparent violent movement. In the middle of a game she could suddenly fall to the ground. Walking long distances would break her legs. Her parents had forbidden her from playing sports or going out onto the street, and when they did allow her, these excursions tended to be brief, punctual rides in the car, which left her with cravings that accumulated into depressive tantrums. In part, those dreams of architecture at home, in which Daniel would become her accomplice, were replacements devised by her brother so that she could experience, no matter how briefly, those other possible lives. Paradoxically, for that same reason, the buildings had a very short life span: Daniel and his sister did not plan for them to last, but rather erected them with an immediate and utilitarian objective—they were stages. He and Sofía used them to perform, with increasing frequency (since it was hard for him to ever say no to her), unbridled and crass theatrical works, variations of classics and fairy tales, hysterical summaries of novels about knights and serial tales of espionage and assassins, or fatal romances with vengeance reaped from beyond the grave, all of which were selected with the patience of a Sufi theologian by the determined little girl, who spent hours rifling through the library-bedroom bookcases to locate the stories, extracting them from the books that abounded in that room, which was, in this way, a home to other uncountable and unconfined rooms.

When a new paper monument had been finished, the siblings would load it onto a small rack and very carefully bring it down the stairway that led to the backyard. There, making sure that their parents were out of sight, they would begin their short theatrical functions: a few quick, nervous acts that intermingled the lives of noble characters with the lives of the fabulously wretched, which inevitably ended in apocalyptic denouements wherein heroes and antiheroes, villains and heartthrobs, virgins and adulterers, zealots and slackers all went up in real flames between the walls and ceilings of those shrunken worlds. Daniel and Sofía performed the dramas, playing each role and accounting for every detail: the victims' shrieks of panic were the girl's specialty, and these she emitted through paper cones that she held in her hands, sometimes aiming them at the fire to send an additional breath of air that would invigorate the flames and precipitate the sacrifice. At the end, they both took great care to put out the fire just before the construction burned beyond all recognition, and then they picked up the rubble, piling the ashes inside the miniature rooms, and carried the remains to the library-bedroom in order to add them to that great model of the damaged city, comprised of the remains of their previous works, with streets and city centers giving way to landscapes, alleys, and dead ends, something that Daniel called, with a wink of perverseness, his "somnambulistic micropolis," in whose blackened curves rose the surviving walls of Hamlet's castle, the jail of Segismundo, and the villa of Triste-le-Roy.

Only once was I granted admittance to one of those private functions. The plot of the mini-farce was the conflicted romance of a couple, a deaf-mute sharecropper and a very young woman, almost a girl. She was the housekeeper of a merchant who sold cheeses and hams wholesale. She and her lover plotted a joint suicide that was thwarted by the man's unexpected, sad immunity to the ingested poison. That time, with papier-mâché, thin copper threads, and lead wire—the stone blocks painted in brown and white watercolors—Daniel and Sofía had constructed the prison where the deaf-mute was locked up for killing his beloved, and they had copied maps and engravings of the prison at Brie where Jean Valjean had paid for his crime. In their story, the young share-cropper (in complicity with a guard given to nocturnal trysts and disposed to grant any favor that offered the promise of provid-ing just that) managed to free himself from his cell. But, instead of escaping, he decided to consummate his unfinished accord, burning himself alive in the side courtyard of one of the prison wards, so that his remains would rise up to the heavens in smoke and seek the ghost of his beloved. When Daniel and Sofía lit the fire—he running and she delicately jogging around the miniature scenery—the voices of the prisoners and guards that they acted out filled the tiny papier-mâché prison and dispersed like meteorites throughout the closed-off backyard: shouts of comic theater, coos of the tragic order, infantile restless giggles that shook the walls of one building and the next, like the bleating of calves trapped under the rubble of a granary that had fallen on top of them. While emitting all the voices of that labyrinthine chorus, Daniel and Sofía would prance around the debris, absorbed by the flashing glow of wickedness, the same shining reflection in their eyes, two children in ecstasy over mischief for which they were responsible, unbeknownst to their parents.

FOUR

But that's not how it is anymore. Now, seated on the floor of the hospital's central courtyard, Daniel seemed to have aged prematurely, with that brown cross on his forehead, patches of wrinkles, and drooping eyes. He remained silent for a while, shamelessly scrutinizing the woman with a piece of bread in her mouth. The air was liquefying and turning gray, and suddenly the fog covered everything.

"After Juliana's death," said Daniel, "the sentence was given, and my mother got them to bring me here instead of the prison, by paying the judge and a couple of psychiatrists whose testimonies were fabricated in view of her requests."

During his first months in the hospital, they had numbed his mind with sleeping pills and antidepressants, had made him sleep week after week (he lost track of how many), and the few images he had from that time could have been dreams or memories.

"They'd get me out of bed to go to the bathroom, make me walk around the room in circles, and they asked me trivialities or answered my questions incoherently."

They had made him eat in bed and sleep for twelve or fourteen hours straight with very brief lapses in between. He had learned to stay in that dreamlike haze in his waking-state, to think of nothing, to stop measuring or distinguishing day from night.

"I realized that I was able to seek out unconsciousness, to deny myself lucidity, to move my entire past life to a single blind spot in order to refrain from reliving each minute of it."

But there were times when he awoke, lost in a gaze at that cloudy stain, black as a bat, that fluttered around his room, and he let it happen for a few seconds when the image of Juliana would suddenly appear, on a highway, her body covered with cuts, scratches, and stab wounds, thirty-six in all: Juliana was a disassembled mannequin in the trunk of his car.

"And I almost immediately realized that I was crying and my shirt was wet, or that I had pissed my pants, and I left my room to beg someone to please give me more pills, but I couldn't speak. By the time the sleep therapy ended, I had lost a lot of weight, and my elbows and clavicle were on the verge of stretching my skin and perhaps even piercing it in an attempt to escape my body. My mother came every day, and some friends—Gálvez and Pastor first, and later on Mireaux visited me somewhat frequently—but we shared the same desire to be face-to-face and yet invisible to each other."

They had continued to wake him slowly, lengthening by minutes and later by hours his wakefulness between days of incoherence, and one morning Daniel thought that perhaps it was true that an error had been made and they now had awoken him from his dream.

"In the beginning they didn't leave me alone for an instant, but stayed right there in the hallway, sat a few yards away and watched me walk through the courtyard, stumbling as I went."

A nurse was always nearby, and at the door to his room a police officer stood guard each morning and would follow him wherever he went: eating with him, accompanying him to the bathroom and on his walks through the ward.

"In those early days, I felt that the other patients were specters, products of my delusion, that I didn't belong in this maze of living gargoyles. I had to be different. I don't recall the first time I squatted in that courtyard, like the others, or exchanged words with one of them, nor could I say what we spoke about. But at a certain moment I realized: no matter who they were, I was just another member of this community—I had the same routines as them, spent my days in a white-out wandering through the hallways and the courtyard, like everyone else, counting the number of leaves remaining on the bushes, entering monosyllabic discussions, without any certainty of the meaning of my words or of anyone else's, but I spoke to them in a subdued tone, barely audible, because speaking with someone reminded me that I was one of them, and I wasn't prepared for that."

So it was that a line of reasoning began to form in his mind, a splinter of sanity that invaded him like an illness.

"I knew that I was transforming into a distant being—not that my thoughts were lacking meaning, but worse, that they had inaccurate or undecipherable meanings for me."

One afternoon, he had wanted to tell his mother, "Bring me some books from the house," but only the word *books* came out, and he had wanted to mention the title of one of them, but he found nothing in his memory.

"Nevertheless, she intuited what I wanted to say. She knew it was a good idea, and the following day she showed up at the hospital with two full boxes and the little bookcase that you've just seen in my room—which now is empty, and shortly you'll know why. I read as if I were possessed, searching for who knows what, sometimes four or five books at a time, trying to replace those nightmares with the stories that I was unearthing in these books. But this wasn't easy. In the beginning each line came with a riddle. I gaped at the words. Not that I was meditating on them, but rather discovering them, looking them in the eyes, as if I'd never had a language before."

Every morning he had fallen on the ground of gravel and sand in the courtyard, beneath the nonexistent shade of the bush, with a pile of books at his side, and the others had learned to respect his silence.

"Once, one of them was perching on the nearby bench, stretching out his neck behind me, and he stayed there for several minutes, several hours, following with his eyes the line of black characters that I was underlining with my finger."

One morning he had spoken to someone, very slowly and so that no one else could overhear, not two or three disconnected words but a complete phrase, with a desire to elicit a real answer.

"He was an elderly fellow with a tense and pallid face, not unlike cardboard, who always remained in his room and was only allowed to visit the courtyard when it was empty, but that day— you try to figure out why!—he lay down next to me and began to build towers and pyramids with my books. I looked at the man compassionately, supportively, and inquired, 'And why, may I ask, have they put you in here?' The man didn't take his eyes off my books, but raised a hand toward the sky, pointing at God knows what with his wrinkled and colorless finger, and said to me, 'No one has put me in here.'"

And then he had lowered his finger to Daniel's face, just in front of his eyes, had moved it around and said something else: "I'm the one who has locked out everyone else, so that they devour each other. If you want to leave this place someday, come speak to me," and for the first time Daniel had felt that the other patients were beings of flesh and bone.

"After that, I grew accustomed to stopping the patients every time my path crossed one of theirs. I'd take them by the arm or motion for them to follow me into the courtyard and, squatting on the ground, I spoke with them."

Two years had passed, as far as he knew, and only then had he learned to accept that he was actually in a psychiatric hospital, and that the zombified creatures who roamed this place, muttering or whispering illogical sentences, canticles in unknown languages, or short phrases repeated thousands of times, as well as grunts and unfinished diatribes wherein the words *hooker, bird, virgin,* and *marriage* would cyclically recur, were mentally ill, not devils or ghosts from a bad dream.

"At a certain moment—before, I know not when, it's all so confusing—I had managed to convince myself that I was in a regular hospital, I mean that those people were *normal* patients and that my delirium had turned them into spooks and chimeras, and I wanted to disguise my plight, so that no one would suspect that I had gone mad."

But slowly recognizing that the place was an asylum made him feel that he was in his right mind, and ever since then, during the third year, things had started to head in a different direction.

"I came to the realization that the books were changing for me. They were no longer accumulations of short phrases with disjointed meanings, shards, particles that gave rise to independent and blurry memories. They now had a defined form, they were stories and accounts with certain direction."

He had begun to recognize certain passages and notions, and to realize that some books pleased him more than others, and to discriminate between them, to accept some and reject others. Without knowing why, he had begun to select the best ones to read aloud, in the courtyard, in the hallway, facing a congregation of mental patients who, squatting, formed a circle around him every afternoon, some gnawing on bread and candy, others letting out warbles, bellowed approvals, or gasps in response to his words.

"I transformed into the high priest of the ogres, with an entourage of angelic loons who listened to my predictions—entranced or indifferent, it doesn't matter—and in a certain way I felt that through them my connection to the world was being reestablished."

And they too, the others, had agreed to close that circle around him, to each occupy a space equal to the rest, though different from Daniel's, and in their gatherings, at the center of the ward, that collection of amorphous men and women, who spoke languages that no one else on earth spoke, had achieved a detestable yet real harmony.

"Shortly thereafter, in their monologues, in the gibberish that they ceaselessly repeated from the crack of dawn to midnight, every day, day after day, tiny apertures began to form and through them there appeared the names of people and places heard in my readings; entire phrases suddenly materialized in paragraphs made of onomatopoeia and reiterations, like an eye emerging in the center of a hurricane."

And the others had laughed at those coincidences, had demonstrated that they recognized them, or at least that's what Daniel thought when he'd notice a guffaw leap from a toothless, fang-studded, or cavity-stricken mouth, when he'd notice a sudden hand-slap of complicity, followed by a moment of perplexity and a gradual return to shock.

"Over time, each person found a fixed spot in the circle, staking claim to one place in particular, and when I sat on the ground and began to read, they shuffled around until finding the right spot and then—twisting their bodies to get settled, their heels together, their hands on their shins, their heads sunken between their knees, their mouths half-open, their eyes blind to everything—they were cadavers of recently exhumed, still dust-covered children who would listen to my readings as if they were a mob that came back to life in a mass grave. Over a couple of months, some stability had arisen from the chaos of the ward, a routine that didn't depend on the hospital rules but on the will of the patients, who seemed to keep secret their awareness of the hours remaining until the next conclave and seemed to reserve their madness for other times of the day, because once they had formed that circle they acted ceremoniously, as if they were being cautious not to violate a higher law and, without looking at me, led me to believe that they were there for my sake, to listen to what I had to say, no matter what it was."

New patients arrived and followed the involuntary habit of withdrawing from everyone else, spending hours and days in bliss staring at a stone, a dead pigeon, a cloud in the shape of a hammer, but incrementally they would be allured, one afternoon, by the convention of mute statues in fetal positions and the voice of their pasty leader, and they too would manage to form part of the circle.

The Antiquarian is a personage cloistered in a tower of books and sun-faded bundles of paper, ever a stranger to the world around him. He reads about the life of the deceased in octavo tomes, printed in venerable languages, and he studies both time and space without exposing himself to the inclemency of either time or space: a prisoner, surrounded by columns of printed paper, illegible scribbles, oriental characters, each moment of humanity available to him in alphabetical order on the walls of his room, with impunity from everything except for his gaze. He has consumed thirty years of his life in this place, whence he escapes by his lonesome after nightfall. With a tome clenched in his hand and a finger saving the page, the Antiquarian most carefully verifies the similarities and differences between the physical world and the world that he knows by memory from the books; the city that he inhabits is changing—each night the number of vagrants on the corners increases, throngs of strangers who flood the avenues or lie down in alleys and side streets, and the Antiquarian registers this metamorphosis with surprise.

FIVE

"Are you sure this is the best way?"

"Psh. This street takes us to the avenue and from there it's a straight shot."

"Well, all right then."

When we were not on our way to his library-bedroom or to the neighborhood of smoke-filled bordellos, Daniel would drag me to what soon became the fifth stage of our younger lives: a little side street parallel to the spiraling avenue, in which, perhaps since time immemorial, six or seven dozen males and females, old folks and children alike, had taken possession of about a quarter mile of the shoulder downtown. They spent all day there, seated atop fruit crates or buckets, rickety stools, or slipshod armchairs, surrounded by colonnades of smoggy, dusty books, mountains of tomes that rose up around their owners like the pillars of a temple whose rooftop had been stolen the night before by some ignorant god, jealous of that distant cult of arts and letters. Nearly every old-time book dealer was acquainted with Daniel, and each offered him rarities and collectors' pieces, or from secret nooks would unveil corpulent volumes with burn marks or the brownish fuzz of some mold cultivated by the moisture of this amphibious city, volumes in which Daniel anticipated findings and surprises that—during those early days, before he had learned the craft of negotiation—made it impossible for him to haggle, and he would inevitably invest every penny that had found its way into his pockets.

With its zigzagging blocks infested with buyers of the most surreptitious of appearances, who strolled amongst the hills of paper with their heads cocked sideways, attempting to decipher the titles on spines aged by perpetual exposure to the sun and fog; and with its unsettling mob of dealers, who were entrenched behind walls of tomes tossed on top of each other or lined up on numerous shelves of makeshift cases fashioned out of wood, stakes, planks, and metal sheets, that Biblio Path, as it had been coined, gave me the curious impression that this world had emerged from a Ray Bradbury novel. As I threaded my way through the twists and turns of that winding road that seemed to ooze books and dealers, I imagined the place as an encampment of refugees sought after by a troop of soldiers that had received the order to extinguish even the last piece of printed paper in the world—an itinerant tribe of outstanding men of culture, martyrs who had taken upon their shoulders the responsibility of saving the history of humanity and founding it again in the form of a library. Amid the book dealers there were two or three women and a couple of girls conversing amongst themselves in the distance, letting out squeals of pleasure or grunts of pain, according to what would befit the stories being told, and beyond them one could perceive the hidden presence of a boy working a nearby stand. Yet, despite the presence of those few women, the place appeared a masculine enclave, dominated by a certain race of youthful, hyperactive merchants who hawked their merchandise, shouting the titles of illustrated opuscules and ecclesiastic encyclopediae as if they were selling mechanical tools or school utensils. But there was likewise a more peaceful group of elderly dealers, almost always nestled on narrow seats of dyed metal like those of a theater, and they would read and underline phrases and paragraphs and would furtively raise their faces to observe everything with their sibylline, unaffected, weary eyes, cataloguing or outlining in their mind the profile of each passerby, each social climber, each pedestrian shopper in the surroundings of those fragile proto-bookstores of mended walls and invisible ceilings, where they spent ten- to twelve-hour spans each day of the week.

As we passed by the numerous tables, Daniel introduced me to many of those vendors of printed antiquities: former fish or vegetable vendors, ex-schoolteachers, licensed policemen retired from hospitals or jails, elderly men exiled from their children's houses, some at night condemned to sleep in the same unsuitable kiosks in which they worked by day. Out of all of these, one captured my imagination with fulminating rapidity: he was a very elderly man with squinty eyes and a flattened forehead. The crown of his head was bald and sunburned, surrounded by patches of shiny hair dyed black, and he wore a kerchief around his neck, a collared shirt, and gray pants. His blazer was hanging on the lintel of his kiosk, and a surprisingly small, dark skull that could have been from a child, or perhaps from a monkey, had been placed upon a table made of cardboard boxes. This elderly man was the only one of the tribe who had once been the proprietor of a real bookstore, but his previous establishment had been lost years ago when the adjoining building, owned by a foreign company, had been blown to pieces by a bomb during the times of the early attacks.

"He's a specialist in obscurities," Daniel said, smiling, when he put us face-to-face for the first time, pronouncing his surname, Yanaúma, and his nickname, Cabecita Negra, and nudging me onto a small chair of damp wood, in a gesture that said "We're going to be here for a while."

On that occasion, Yanaúma discoursed for hours on end, with a patient yet colorful voice, digressing with random details and erupting into perverse stories whose actors, in each and every case, were not human beings as much as they were ideas—two ideas to be specific, and the links between them: Death and Books. In spite of the superabundance of dates and proper names, toponyms and arcane allusions to mystics, heretics, and prosecutors of heterodoxies, or to titles of and references to legendary editions of oeuvres that had not been read since the dawn of modernity, or that had been censored by some indeterminable power during recent centuries, the pleasant expression of Daniel's one repeating ephemeral smile made me understand that Yanaúma was no novice in the art of yarn-spinning. What he said was, in any case, stunning and terrifying. And out of everything he mentioned that afternoon, I have saved in my memory the feats in the life of Dr. Magnus Schwarzkopf, one of the hundreds of German angels of death who, during the years of the Final Solution, discovered certain creative talents that had until that time lain dormant.

Schwarzkopf was one of the three surgeons in charge of the experimental rooms in the eleventh ward of the Birkenau concentration camp, known as Auschwitz II, in the suburb of Zasole, on the outskirts of the Polish city of Oświęcim. "Like many others," Yanaúma said, underscoring the incomprehensible coincidence, "Schwarzkopf also had the idea of processing the skin of dead prisoners to manufacture it into paper"—not a hard scroll like the coarse and hollow lamp shades that the North Americans had exposed in the Nuremberg trials, but paper, the most delicate and softest sheets of human paper, almost transparent, though not so much as to allow the writing to become illegible: whitish folios of paper useful for the production of certain luxurious books, which Schwarzkopf had dreamed would populate that pristine world on the brink of coming into fruition. Once he was able to confirm that the dried and tumorous skin of a cadaver, dead perhaps before its proprietor was deceased, was of no use for his product, Schwarzkopf swayed the high commanders of Birkenau to grant him the guardianship of one hundred recently arrived healthy adults, whom he proceeded to eliminate in concert with the progress of the experiment, until he was able to perfect the technique and manufacture resplendent volumes, on the pages of which a group of inmates, professionals and students—utilizing an ink made of the same cadavers used to construct the paper—in cautious but virile gothic calligraphy transcribed the texts of the books that Schwarzkopf placed each morning upon their desks: a version of the Bible in Sanskrit; German translations of Shakespeare; a peculiar edition of *Don Quixote* in Macaronic Latin; all the engravings in de Bry's body of work, assigned to the most capable artist of the camp; the *History* of Saxus Germanicus; *Faustus* and *Reineke Fuchs* by Goethe; and Schwarzkopf's own correspondence with a young philosopher from Danzig (who had been enthusiastically introduced to him). Between the years of 1942 and 1945, the doctor produced his work, ever demanding the provision of new prisoners, transforming his patients into books, removing them from the putrid platforms in the barracks so that he might place them on the shelves of a personal library that continued to grow with vigor. On May 1, 1945, when only one man and one woman were left in the room—siblings, one of whom was shortly to be condemned to write upon the skin of the other—Schwarzkopf passed them a file of handwritten papers which detailed this story and proceeded to bid them farewell with a kiss on the cheek, only to later enter his office and shoot himself in the head. "The library," concluded Yanaúma, with an enigmatic tone, "had been confiscated by the Russians and placed on the black market in 1953, when it was apparently purchased from Stalin by a philanthropist whose check was sent from someplace in South America."

Yanaúma would produce stories like this one without any effort, recalling them or composing them on the fly, with the fluidity of a Provençal troubadour and an overtone of mundane, at times grotesque, malignancy, and he went on erratically attributing them to historians and encyclopedists who could not have known these stories; and, in an imperceptible way, after concluding one of them, he would place the next book on his little cardboard table, declaring that it was indispensable, and would then jump into another story, and after a couple of hours, an accumulation of tomes waited to be priced and delivered to Daniel, a shopper of comprehensive disposition, ever willing to carry any book that might serve as an origin, be it tangential or capricious, of the elderly man's morbid tales.

Just when we were about to leave, Yanaúma rifled through a plywood trunk hidden under the table and pulled out a slim volume with a scandalous cover: in red letters it read *The Fall of the House of Usher, Illustrated Edition*. He said, "Now I know this edition is of interest, but don't let this gift startle you, since it's not intended for you, but for your little sister. Give it to Sofía, and perhaps one day you could bring her here."

We left, dodging vociferous vendors and tripping over mounds of identical copies of books on closeout. "Happy reading," said Yanaúma in the distance, "and don't forget to visit your friend Cabecita Negra."

Then Daniel asked me if I had noticed the little dark skull on the table. "It was the first thing I saw," I said, and Daniel took me by the arm and began enumerating each of the twelve skulls at the entrance of numerous kiosks.

"They're a sign," he said, "a symbol that certain people are meant to comprehend."

"A sign for what?" I asked, without disguising the fact that his cloak-and-dagger attitude was beginning to unnerve me. And then Daniel told me the other half of the story of the old-time book dealers.

"Some of them," he said, "partake of business dealings beyond the sphere of books, and the skull is an ad hoc sign for those who purchase their merchandise. It's a small network, a dozen people at most, that comprise the sentry box of a mafia that traffics in human body parts. Don't look at me like that—this isn't some horror story. Med students need those parts for their practicals, and the universities can't afford to provide them. Just between you and me, not many people are willing to donate their organs—much less their whole body—while they're living, so that they can be used once they're dead, and the medical departments boil over with an excess of students far greater than any effort they make to provide them with the materials they require. The only corpses that can be used are those that the morgue gives them, but that's only when a cadaver is declared unidentifiable, and after days have passed without anyone claiming it. The few corpses that pass through that process arrive at the campus on the verge of decomposition, and there they are attacked by dozens of students who lurk over them like vultures, a cannibalistic crowd, quartering them up in no time at all, transforming them into unrecognizable shreds in a matter of minutes. If a student wants to work at his leisure on an arm, a leg, a head, a heart that still retains its human form, he has to purchase it himself. The only way to obtain such an exclusive artifact is to reserve the body part, and that's why they come here, to find the vendors, who always have that dark skull placed in some visible location in their kiosks, and they make binding agreements with them, which include their complete identification as medical students and, two days later, a ride in a van with a blindfold on to a house somewhere in the city, where they pick up their order. For those times, they better have taken some container adequate for the job; because if they haven't, they run the risk of being abandoned in the middle of a street with a plastic bag containing a kidney, a liver, or perchance a head with a contorted face, eyes wide open, and a petrified sneer."

We traversed the two remaining blocks in silence, Daniel balancing the pile of recently acquired books, the one by Poe on top, intrigued by my terrified reaction to his story, while I tried to discover some feature of malignancy in the merry, dutiful, and indifferent faces of the vendors that would allow me to identify them prior to casting my gaze on their tables, amongst their books, at the door to their kiosks in search of the blackened little skull from a child or a monkey (who knew?) which was the insignia of that trafficking ring that used secondhand bookstores as a front. I never saw anything in their faces that appeared different from the rest.

Over the course of time, when it became clear that the friend-ship between Daniel and Yanaúma would transcend the street-fair atmosphere of books, and when the old man started to become a habitual figure in The Circle, or would suddenly appear prowling amidst bookcases and shelves in the library-bedroom, or sealing secret deals with my friend, their relationship became increasingly unpleasant for me, but also more understandable, for I never did manage to dissociate Yanaúma from the image of the skull and its hidden meaning.

SIX

"One day," continued Daniel, "a girl arrived at the hospital; she must have been sixteen or seventeen, small and dark-skinned, had an empty gaze, always wearing a multicolored cloth wrapped around her back, one end stretching over her right shoulder and the other over her left, and knotted at her breast, as if she were bearing the weight of a child that wasn't there. During the first days, the girl had uttered a single word, *Huk,* one long syllable that seemed to come from a hollow and fibrous instrument, which she pronounced cautiously whenever anyone drew near her: *Huk,* when a caretaker grabbed her by the arm to lead her to the cafeteria or to the commons; *Huk,* each time a patient scrutinized her with the infectious horror of a lunatic's eyes. Save for those rare moments, her customary countenance was dazed and distant, most of all when, for no apparent reason, she'd untie the cloth from her back and lay it on the ground, in one corner of the courtyard or another, and would then curl into a ball upon it, rest her head on a brick, her plastic sandals sticking to the soles of her feet with a patina of dried sweat, and whimper for hours until falling asleep."

That had lasted for weeks, and from a certain moment henceforth, during the meetings of the hospital circle, in the firm gazes and nervous gestures of his audience—that cast of marionettes with twisted bodies and gaunt faces, squatting around his pile of books—Daniel had begun to perceive how the young girl was being recruited into the group, as all of the others had been.

"For that reason, one afternoon I went to have a word with her, took her a handful of cookies, and sat down a couple of feet away from her in the hallway, facing door number one, which was hers, and I asked her, 'What's your name?' and she turned to look at me and remained silent, sitting on the ground, her hands clasped under her bent knees, and then after a few seconds she muttered '*Huk*,' slowly, in her acidic voice, and she said nothing else, but she did allow her murky eyes to rest upon me for an extended period of time, and I felt their touch."

After that day they fell into the routine of sitting down right there, four or five feet from each other, every morning, without even a glance or a word, each against a wall, in the semi-penumbra of the ward, the feet and legs of other patients traveling between them, the sprints of the nurses, someone's shrieks, the clicking of doors that would open and close every so often, the spiderweb of odors of ether and alcohol, the imbroglio of groans, slivers of an incongruent voice splintering off from the rest, rising up above the two of them, forming a pyramid of sounds that floated throughout the hallway and suddenly dissipated in a vacuous and expected silence; and then it came time again to form the circle in the courtyard and make way for the ritual of reading.

"But she never went near the others, and when I took my position at the head of the troop of phantasms, opening the chosen book to repeat the lines that had concluded the last reading and baste them with lines for today, she exited that tendril of the hallway and walked to the opposite corner of the courtyard, only to lie down on her multicolored cloth, and I envisioned the other half of her mind, emerging from afar, joining the dead-faced spooks in my audience. The stories I read were consuming me, were pushing her away, were transforming all of us, that's what I thought, transforming me and everyone else: a patrol of soldiers crawling through the streets of a village, the scream of a child in the darkness, the door of a house in flames, a dog hanged from a lamppost, the bustle of an army of strangers, twenty-five people standing together in a hole in the ground, a group in uniforms aiming their rifles ten yards away. The stories unfolded, materialized before us, before me and my court of awestruck spirits."

One morning, the girl took the five steps that for five weeks had separated her from Daniel. She said *Huk* to him and offered him her hand, a white scar on the palm, curved like the beak of a gull, fingernails bitten, and she got him to walk to her room of unwashed walls, door number one, spread her multicolored cloth on the ground, pointing to it with her finger, and repeated her only word, but now as a question: *Huk?*

"I never knew what she was asking me, or if she was awaiting a response, or if she thought I could somehow answer her. On the other hand, I felt that from then on a bridge connected our two isles of terror, and that someday, who knows, perhaps one of us would be able to cross it. We'd walk together through the hallway, or skirting the benches or the courtyard with its two bushes, we'd enter the common room and from time to time the rooms of other patients, shadows wandering through the shadows, she holding my hand and gazing at the walls and the ceilings with earnestness, scrutinizing them, like a sleepwalker groping a plaster wall in search of the entrance to a secret passageway that would return her to a waking state."

They were together every hour of the day, every day, but Daniel had never managed to convince her to enter the circle: the fallen angels on that end of the courtyard, their wings folded up against their spines, and she at the other end, witnessing the necromancy in awe.

"I can't explain the following with complete accuracy. In a certain way, the presence of the girl, the long stints of silence, my disposition for watching her, for watching her watch me, hour upon hour, got me to understand that the time had come for me to tell my own story."

Between those timeless withdrawals to the hallway and the atrophied solemnity of afternoons in the circle, between the undaunted response of her peers and the cemeterial air that came over the courtyard and ward after sundown, Daniel had decided to return to the highway, to Juliana's body and the thirty-six stab wounds, to meet that moment again—it had been nearly three years since he had transformed into a ghost of himself and been damned to bear this distant life.

"I wanted to string the facts together, to convert them into a sequence of causes and effects. I was a killer—many people knew that; no one knew why—and I wanted to confess my motives to her, perhaps because I believed she wouldn't understand, or rather that only she might be able to understand. Yet, each time I started to say something, the girl would look at me with her startled eyes and say '*Huk,*' and I understood that as 'Don't put words between us.' That's why I decided to tell my story by other means. I spent hours alone by the light of the oil lamp, annotating my memories, reconstructing each apex of remembrance, giving it a space and a form, wont to find someone who would read my papers or listen to what they said, to close this other circle, and I set out to compose a text made of snippets and memories, a farce, a puppet show that was merely the front for a tragedy."

Then, one day, while kneeling amidst the fresh infernal air that surrounded him in the courtyard, Daniel began to confess his story, alternating his fragments with the passages from the book he had chosen for that week, and now, pronouncing each word with difficulty, invoking them in his memory, pounded out by that histrionic minstrel rhythm of his, which had once flourished into his incendiary games with Sofía, Daniel repeated to me what he had told them, in a long tale made of codes and allusions which brought an end to our conversation that afternoon.

The Antiquarian reads: A policeman arrives at a town between two lakes, the sky a reflection of the land, and he walks down the only street, which is empty, searching for a place to eat, and he sees that all the houses of this town are recently extinguished pyres, ash and charcoal, except for the threshold of each door, and likewise he sees that from each lintel there hangs a cadaver: bodies as black as the ruins around them, their necks entangled in knots and wires, and beneath each body a couple of children strive to reach the feet of those who have been hanged. It is time for cleanup, life in this place should begin again, thinks the policeman, moved, and he decides to stay there and live; he adopts the children and reconstructs the houses and, one day, months later, he sees on the mountainside a black string made of moving points that descends toward the town; they are his old comrades and this realization fills him with joy, and he signals to them and, when the column of guards reaches the height of the houses, he is the first to take their bullets, and then they carry his body and hang it from the lintel of a door, light it on fire, and when the men march off, the man dangles there, a blotch of drudgery seeping into the blue sky, and a couple of children attempt to pull him down. Sighing, the Antiquarian closes the book.

SEVEN

"Is this route always so slow?"

"Depends on the time of day. On this road it sometimes seems like your life is passing you by, and other times it's as though there isn't anyone else in the world."

In those now distant years at the university, one singular event divided the waters of Daniel's life. We had spent the evening and part of the night with the book dealers on the Biblio Path, inhaling paper and bacteria and rifling through bookshelves, until there wasn't a penny left in our pockets. So we had walked from there to his house, following the spiraling avenue and watching the city change color and texture, as if it were emerging incrementally from the bottom of a swamp, houses and buildings covered by greenish mildew and black mold spattered on the gates and awnings. On the corners profiles of policemen were dissolving in their sand-colored trench coats, dogs evaporating in the streets, madmen vanishing on the sidewalk, prostitutes and transvestites in the intersections. Also disappearing were buildings with broken windows, walls tagged with graffiti, piles of garbage; everything was replaced by landscapes of weeds and dying gardens, houses wrapped in barbed wire and high-tension nets, condos subdued by straitjackets, homes that held electric shocks—from the street very rarely could a lit lamp or silhouette of a moving shadow be seen inside.

"Do you see them?" asked Daniel, whose neighbors had always been an interesting conversation topic.

"I see them," I said.

"It's like they're not there," he went on, "as if they were images projected on the glass from some point here outside. As far as I can tell, they're holograms. It's a miracle they don't appear upside down, reflections on the retina." He cranked his neck like someone who is about to jump on a trampoline. "They lock themselves in and think that this will guarantee their survival. They await judgment day and expect God to destroy the universe, but leave their houses intact. And since they're afraid of dying, they bury themselves in these gargantuan coffins of concrete and aluminum and spend their whole lives there, staring at the faces of the other lost souls who are their parents, children, and spouses. I say it because this is what my family is like, and I imagine I'm like this too." Daniel walked on, rubbing the palms of his hands on his knuckles: a haggard, pensive, human fly. "Speaking of this," he said, "have you ever heard about the hotels for the dead in Munich?"

We turned onto his street, hearing the hysterical wail of a fire engine and, shortly thereafter, the bustle and bedlam of an army of young men in red and yellow suits. We saw ladders and axes and two streams of water like two geysers detonating through the second-floor windows, and a solid cylinder of light that seemed to shine down from the dead sky over Daniel's house, and inside rooms were being annihilated in a tube of smoke that ascended toward the clouds. For an instant, Daniel stayed at my side and we remained paralyzed and unresponsive, but he suddenly ran and entered the house, tripping over the rubble of doors and furniture and guillotined window frames, and amidst striding pirouettes he disappeared behind the curtain of flaming scarlet waves. Fear turned my skin to stone, and in my chest, hands, and tear-filled eyes, I felt the burn of Hell. Over the hissing of hoses I heard a chorus of moans, hundreds of wild banshees or ghosts, the shrieking of caged birds, all burning alive, and I noticed that a wall on the first floor next to the front door was slowly collapsing, opening up in its center a crack wide enough to stick a hand through. Then that wall collapsed and there was an explosion, a sphere of vapor covered everything for an instant, and a brief silence fell, only to break when two firemen emerged from the blaze, one with a languid, skinny body in his arms, the body of a girl, her flesh exposed. Just a second later, after studying the features of a face that was no longer there, I realized that it was Sofía, Daniel's sister.

I went up to the fireman who was carrying her and I saw the girl's closed eyes, her hands crossed upon her stomach, and I told the fireman that my friend was still inside. The man laid Sofía on the ground amidst a balustrade of legs and ran toward the house. A paramedic came and opened her mouth, plugged her nose, and she arched her back and pushed air past her lips. Olga, an elderly woman who had been Daniel's nanny, was sitting on the sidewalk across the street, her face dark with soot and her skirt torn to her thighs. Two children on bicycles rode around her in circles, making faces of fright or disgust, and they watched her like someone who observes a dead body. A policeman took her by the arms and helped her to a patrol car, where a fifteen-year-old girl sat on the hood, looking at the fire without batting an eyelash. I got down on my knees in the grass to see Sofía, still immobile, the flare of her Cinderella skirt trampled by the cops and firemen, and one of them suddenly gave her a sharp blow to the chest and Sofía's body convulsed and her neck twisted toward me, while from her mouth there dripped a black and brown drool, thick like a liquid of half-pureed spiders. Her jaw trembled; the skin under her eyes was an orange film covered with sores, her hair a nest of frayed threads. Sofía turned her face to the house and then to me, staring right through me, her gums calcined behind her limp lips, her

her sides in laughter, with a glow of innocence in her eyes and a ballet of orange and yellow flames closing in on her, and even though Olga had endeavored to draw near the door again and had taken a couple of steps inside, a high shelf of burning dolls and puppets above the threshold had fallen on her, forcing her to leave, petrified.

A few articles had appeared in the newspapers that attributed the fire to a terrorist attack, linking the event to Daniel's father's refusal to pay extortion to a subversive group. Daniel told me about this rumor between inexplicable chuckles, since he was the victim of a talkative depression that led him to tell the story of that night as if it were a distant, anodyne tale.

According to the other maid, Sofía had waited for Daniel all afternoon, sitting on the bed of the library-bedroom, rehearsing monologues and speeches that, indubitably, were going to be part of that day's comedy, and readying the scale model of a clock tower which was to be the ritual pyre of the culminating scene. After hours, so it seemed, bored and ill-tempered, belting out curses and obscenities in the voice of a cartoon character, which alarmed Olga—but not enough to make her go see what was happening— Sofía had gone down to the basement, lost in one of those hymns of hers that projected piss and vinegar at anyone in earshot, and the only discernible word, according to the chauffeur, who saw her down there, had been *Daniel,* which she pronounced with rage. From the basement, she had carried the mock-up of the house, of *that* house in which they used to live—"Home is where the hearth is," said Daniel with melancholy—and she had taken it to her bedroom, stomping up the stairs from the basement, through the garage, to the first and then the second floor, and she had lit it on fire. It was that fire of the microcosmic house that had burned the real house to the ground.

As days went by, Daniel ceased speaking of Sofía more and more, and he seemed to avoid his memory of her at all cost, even when the shadow of the girl virtually materialized. More than once, I asked him about her and he did not utter a word, or he refused to drop his current topic, no matter what it was.

One day it occurred to me (I don't know why) to remind him of that night, when we saw the first glimmers of the fire just as he had finished asking me a question: "Have you ever heard about the hotels for the dead in Munich?"

Daniel thought for a second. "Sure, I was going to tell you that when we saw the flames. Well," he said, and he reclined on the pillows of his bed and spoke, adjusting his voice to the character of the story: "In nineteenth-century Munich a peculiar epidemic, or rather, a collective psychosis had spread. There was a series of incidents drawn straight from a gothic novel, people who died and, suddenly, one or two days later, halfway through the funeral ceremony at their own wakes or burials, amid relatives dressed in black, arose from their caskets with baffled and sorrowful expressions, wondering what kind of demented, vicious joke was being played on them. Grumbling, they then left for their houses to finish what they'd started before death had become of them. They were diagnosed with a fleeting coma, epilepsy, severe but momentary catatonia, this being the intriguing yet random feature that each patient shared. Even though the doctors tried to give an explanation, people understood them as diabolical or, perhaps, divine omens. It was all the same because, in every case, they demonstrated that death was a deceitful and fragile state, perchance short-lived at times, and for that reason the phenomenon gave rise to a preventative fever of inventors who designed sarcophagi with horns and bells, so that the dead might alert the living from the underground in the event of a tardy resurrection.

So graves were dug with an escape hatch, and coffins were assembled with drums for Morse code and with telegraphic lines connected to the surface, and, at the apogee of this necrophobic euphoria, someone conceived of the idea of the *Leichenhauser:* hotels for the dead. At first they were small estates stocked with food and equipped with water wells, furnished bedrooms, parlors, and bathrooms, where the corpses of the dearly departed were deposited for a sensible period of time, between two weeks and two months, with the hope that they'd come back to life and find what they might need to revitalize and regain their strength, so that one day they could jump into a wagon and drive their horses toward the city. Soon thereafter, the lapses grew longer and the places became more sophisticated. Around 1865, some chronicler came to say—exaggerating, but not all that much—that the zone of the *Leichenhauser,* to the southwest of Munich, occupied an area similar in dimensions to that of the old heart of the city, with chicken coops and three-story mansions and two or three concentric circles of cobblestone streets, and that at the doors of the houses skeletons of mules and dead horses were stationed, with the hope that their phantasmal owners might one morning open the door and mount up in order to escape those nightmarish streets. There was a road that connected the two settlements, Munich and the land of the dead, and the pedestrians who crossed one another's paths, walking in opposite directions, never knew if the person who greeted them was a mortal-in-the-making or a corpse on its triumphant return. They were all the same; no one was able to distinguish death from its shadow, that projection of death, which was the life of the living."

Olga, crossing herself at every other word, was the first to tell me in detail what had happened to Sofía, and this was almost a year after the fact. Even though the girl survived the fire, the burns consumed much of her face. They marked her limbs and increased the innate fragility of her muscles, and her demeanor as a rebellious, playful, and sometimes irascible little girl vanished into a sinister, mortifying silence, twice as atrocious for those who lived with her, because she never removed that infantile, blissful smile I had seen on the night of the fire and that now was smeared onto her featureless face, raising her nurses' hair on end and giving her visitors goose bumps.

The only time she had said a word to anyone, she had said it to Daniel, in front of her parents: "Now my bedroom is the center of the world, and *you* are going to be my assistant. I already have the list of the damned in writing."

And that same night the family had decided that as soon as she left the hospital, Sofía would have to go into some sort of home. In the days that followed, her mother, after visiting all the places recommended by the psychiatrists, had chosen a residence for rich children on the outskirts of the city, a bewitched miniature palace with stone walls, three rows of slanted rooftops, and arching windows, whose inhabitants consisted of two dozen blond, red, dark-haired, crippled cherubs, victims of bizarre evils, incapable of tying their shoes or looking in a mirror, and amongst them Sofía roamed wearing a white veil that she raised only to frighten the others with a perennial smile and a forefinger outstretched to formulate a wordless question each time someone grew fascinated by her anarchic contortions and managed to rouse her anger. And only after instilling one of those abstract, fleeting panics in one of her little cloistered peers would Sofía seem to recuperate her temperament; she'd attempt to take a few lively steps in the garden, she'd sing the stanza of one of her old incendiary chants, and she'd lean against a tree, hugging it with both arms in an embrace of

joviality that soon waxed anguish, and she'd freeze there in such
a way that the figure of the red and brown girl, laminated with
wounded skin and elastic scars, seemed to form a union with the
trunk, to be part of it, and when the nurses would attempt to re-
move her, to untangle her from that embrace that could have lasted
for hours, to return her to the house, the women would shudder
upon hearing the fibrous crunching of her frail bones as they broke,
her muscles tearing in two. Each incident was followed by many
long days in bed, and Sofía saw them pass without moving, her
invariable smile and eyes locked on the flight of the mosquitoes that
arrived, lost in the streams of sunlight, to smash into the screen of
her window, and while she was in that position, her bones began
to fuse together, her joints to fit a bit farther there or here from
where they were before, and her muscle tissue to reattach itself,
a bit shorter or longer than before; and a few weeks later, when
Sofía finally sat up and slid down from the bed, her posture was a
tad more hunched, stranger than before, and her movements all
the more shocking.

The end of the story I myself would judge implausible had I
not verified its appearance in several newspapers: Sofía had been
living in that limbo of angelic automatons over four or five years,
when one morning the shift nurse went to wake her up with the
intention of helping her change her clothes, as is a daily custom
there, and accompanying her to breakfast with the other patients;
but she found the bed empty and, on the night table, manufactured
with scrupulous care, she discovered a small wax paper house,
the windows and doors delineated by crayons, alongside a box of
matches and a card signed *Sofía,* with a fat dot over the *i,* written
in red marker, like a devilish drop of blood and seemingly in the
shape of a heart. From the time of that exit, which some believed

to be a kidnapping, others an escape, and still others suicide or homicide, Daniel's silence about his sister turned hermetic and definitive, and throughout these fifteen years, even the times in which a crystalline glow moistened his eyes and it was evident to me that the image of Sofía had drained back into his memory, he never said anything, and I never dared to ask.

EIGHT

"I still need to get you up to speed," continued Daniel the follow-ing afternoon in the hospital, a light fog outside, a string of drool dangling from his lower lip. "I have some news to tell you. Who would've thought that my life could get worse? But it has, and that's why I called you."

With his hands pressed against the ground of the courtyard, Daniel unfolded his body, stood up, and began to walk into the hol-low hallway, his hands and legs possessed by an unwavering tremor, like the ringing of a recently pressed piano key. I walked behind him, back inside, toward the yellow light of his room, where I found myself once again in the chair, he once again on the floor. He then explained to me the reason for his call the previous day.

"That time," he said, "when I finished reading my story, and the circle dissolved as it does every night, unconscious noises started seizing the patients' mouths after their momentary hiatus from madness, and they went on to evaporate behind the doors of their rooms. Nothing out of the ordinary, just routine in the ward."

But Daniel had stayed in the courtyard thinking about the meaninglessness of his tales: "The others had heard them while hardly altering their expressions, which were now quite deformed by their illnesses: schizophrenia and psychosis left traces, hiero-glyphics impossible to modify. Their faces were papers teeming with writings, crammed with indefinable references, and any new emotion was lost in the palimpsest of scribbles that the disorder had drawn on them. I was sitting there for quite a while," Daniel said, "I don't know how long. I felt sad, with the paradoxical impression that I had detached too soon from the only thing that was totally mine, and that I had done so illogically, blindfolded, using words that wouldn't express or even protect me, words that rose up like a mural in my consciousness from my subconsciousness, and only when I finally got to my feet with the intention of returning to my room did I realize that someone else was still in the courtyard. Lying on her multicolored cloth, her head resting on a brick, her eyes full of tears, moaning in a subdued voice: '*Huk.*'"

Daniel had seen the young woman, almost a girl, still awake, and had the somewhat ridiculous idea that she had actually understood his story: how else could that moaning be explained, her hands crossed upon her breasts, containing, he had thought, the deepest of sympathies, which then traveled to the sides of her head and, with her skinny fingers, those little rodent claws, she dug at her ears, as if she wanted to extract from her mind the recently registered words.

"I sat at her side," said Daniel. "It was foggy, like it is today; the air was wet. I put a hand upon her hands, giggled, and said, 'There now, they're just stories, histories, words, they're not important,' and while I was speaking I wasn't sure what to think, or if I was happy about the suspicion that someone might have understood me—was this finally the bridge between the isles of terror? Or maybe, instead, I was stricken with grief, worn out, or empty. That's what it was—not only had I left my story, the story was hers now, it was Huk's. She felt it more vividly than I, as more real, and she suffered. Something I, stuffed with pills at first and forced to forget, had never managed to do."

That had occurred two weeks ago; the insane masses of the circle had continued each afternoon, the cast of hysterical figures

squatting in an arc around Daniel, his stories populated with soldiers and vigilantes, hordes of peasants, terrorists, people who
were marginalized and displaced, migrants, the crippled, the blind,
in fables that were woven into the fraying threads of other fables,
which the girl always consumed in groans, curled up in the farthest
corner of the courtyard.

"But, each evening, as the circle dispersed, I noticed that something was transforming. Groups of patients were staying huddled
on the ground, in squalid bunches of shadows, exchanging mum-
bles and grunts, or they scattered only to gather again behind the
bench, sheltered by the main door, standing atop patches of grass
at the edge. It was as if they were discussing, negotiating deals in
a language that suddenly became communicative."

Every time Daniel had discovered them, splinters of *their*
phrases, which were detached from the stories that *he* had read
to them at one time or another, had jumped up in his face: *Memory
closes in upon itself, like the coiling of a serpent,* he heard one time.
The snail shell of your ear is as tiny as a bullet hole, he understood
one morning, and another evening he heard, *It's me, an object on
this side: a rape machine.* And later, *Tanned and dried and sliced with
finesse, you'd make fine paper.* But always, at the end of each phrase,
sensing that they'd been discovered, the patients had turned their
heads toward him, and upon seeing him had closed their mouths
with a hurried, automatic expression and violently submerged
once more into their jungle of silences.

"They walked through the courtyard, as always, letting their
eyes wander toward the tiled cement blocks, but suddenly, at any
moment, three or four of them would cram together to form a
huddle. It didn't matter where, their voices reached every corner
of the hospital. *The cemetery is so large it encroaches on the streets,* I
understood one time. Sometimes laughter made of bleats and

gurgles interrupted a phrase, often I didn't manage to see anybody, but I sensed the patter of footsteps vanish down the hall, laughter scuttling along, and I ran behind it, to find the row of white and gray doors always closed, mischievous snorts behind them. *I am blind, but I saw Juan, the absent brother,* I heard, and traced my own footsteps, went out to the courtyard of gravel and sand, spent hours thinking under the nonexistent shade of the tree, and once one of the patients shouted from somewhere in the ward, *You had to murder the woman who loved you.* And then, in the mortal laxity of the hospital, the wind blew over the moss on the bricks, and I waited for the hours to pass until nightfall, *the silent field,* when my enemies would leave their hiding places, put different faces on, and take to their places around me to hear my words."

One evening, the Antiquarian leaves his tower to take a walk through the city, following a long and winding road that continues to close in on itself, like the coiling of a serpent, and as he goes, his face is stuck in his tomes, lost in a book of fiction or one of history, it's all the same: the Antiquarian reads the legend of a megalomaniac who divides the poor people of a kingdom into two armies and then convinces them to kill one another. There comes the succession of minuscule battles and at the end of the final combat the tyrant remains alone in the center of an orchard or a cemetery. And reading this, the Antiquarian knocks on the door of a house, or perhaps a motel, it's hard to say, and sees a woman barely visible in the window amidst artificial flowers, and there's music, and the sound of other people behind her, and he hears her say Hello, come with me, and he looks at the woman reverently, without suspicion, for a while, and then he walks away.

NINE

"Here we are, better late than never."

"Do you have change?"

"A good cabby never has change."

Not many years ago, the building that houses *La Verdad*—three narrow adobe stories with worn wooden balconies and stained-glass windows sullied by birds that perched on its sills before swooping over passersby—became almost invisible amidst the shadows of the adjoining buildings and the double barricade of cement bags and police cars. As still happens to this day, at any time of day, a sea of downcast strangers would cross the street, in a hurry or indecisively, with the demeanor of soldiers traversing a field after a battle and fearing that, at any moment, enemies pretending to be dead could jump up and pierce them with bayonets.

Sebastian Mireaux, CEO and founder of the newspaper, is a conservative and aristocrat, making him a strange bird in a society where, according to him, being a conservative means defending a moronic, half-breed, mediocre bourgeoisie, which of course is the aristocracy's worst nightmare. During the most violent years, the newspaper did not change the arrogant, aggressive attitude that made it a virtual opponent of 99 percent of the country, and it attacked the government and political parties with the same acrimony as it attacked unions and subversive groups, which is why it was hard to say which of these rivals was responsible for the two explosions that blew to smithereens the newspaper's garage, warehouse, and stained-glass windows in the front room. It now is seen as an architectural miracle that the central structure and the two minarets remain standing; however, as the editors, photographers, and secretaries say, the greater mystery is that Mireaux, the first member of The Circle, a little man over seventy years who walks hunched over like a hook, is still able to climb the eighty steps each morning that lead from the sidewalk to that pentagonal office of his that crowns the building, a discreet yet authoritarian work-place, where one feels the unsettling, disproportionate presence of a certain angular, asymmetric object that occupies half of the space and that appears to be some kind of piano, veiled by a white sheet. The walls are infested with photographs that flaunt all of his phases of physical decadence: Mireaux as a boy with ministers and ambassadors in another lifetime, as a young man with a wife who passed away long ago, as an adult with a child who seems to be older than he, as a geezer with that little niece of his whose linguistic difficulties I had treated a while back. It was there that I visited him, without scorn but also without friendliness, when I saw him a few days ago, after my long conversation with Daniel (which I needed to continue the following afternoon), with the idea of talking to him about my friend and about Juliana.

She and Daniel had met at the newspaper. He would come early on Wednesday mornings to deliver his opinion columns to Mireaux. They were strange miniature opuses in which, defying the conventional prudence of the press, Daniel turned other people's theories on their heads in order to explain, through the artifice of some timeless quote, the complex system of escalating crime rates and acts of vengeance which, so he said, was the history of humanity. Mireaux was happy to publish them, imagining the commotion that so-and-so would suffer upon reading them. Juliana, at that time, would have been twenty-three. She had recently finished a Fine Arts degree and the job at the newspaper was her first. She occupied a beautiful, simple office on the ground floor, with a large rectangular table lit by a light on a thin boom arm, covered with jars of paint, brushes, and reams of white paper and card stock, with a small conical lamp on each surface, and her only responsibility was to produce the illustrations that accompanied the editorial opinion essays. For this reason, she often had to ask Daniel for clarifications about the content of those euphoric, Rabelaisian articles, which he would explain to her by slipping in the most far-out and arbitrary of examples, and smiling here and there, with a nervous tremble in his hands and voice, in such a way that she, a sensible yet anesthetized woman, owner of a guilty indolence that made her resistant to any strain on the imagination, was always left doubting whether this guy was an expendable lunatic who was assigned the column out of Mireaux's pity or humor, or if, on the contrary, Daniel was one of those ironic cases in which a striking intelligence is inexplicably granted to a person whose connections to others are atrophied, a sweaty deaf-mute who suddenly vaults over some crippling silence by unleashing spectacular vociferations, without anyone's ever being able to perceive the springs that enabled him to take that unforeseen leap.

Over the last three years, I hadn't withdrawn only from Daniel, but also from his closest friends, afraid that they would reproach me for having abandoned him after his breakdown and Juliana's murder. Now, however, after my visit to the hospital, after Daniel's long important story, which explained little and had left me in foggy shock, I felt the immediate need to make up for lost time. It was as though Daniel's story, plastered with hidden snippets and coded messages, had sparked me awake in the way of certain therapies for people who repress their emotions. After years had slipped away, I suddenly felt an urgency to speak about Daniel and hear what his friends had to say about him and his relationship with Juliana. And I thought that my initial contact should be with someone who had been present when the couple first got together, and who had also felt a certain affection for her; someone who, at the time of the crime, would have undoubtedly been on the verge of renouncing all contact with him, as I did. Mireaux was not surprised by my presence, nor was he overwhelmed when I explained my motives for visiting him; he was quick to travel back in time and tell me what he recalled.

"One morning, during their early years," said Mireaux, divulging secrets that Juliana herself had told him in confidence, "she had left the office sooner than usual, walked two blocks to where her car was parked, and when she got there, she had seen Daniel sitting on a bench in the neighboring park, surrounded as always by a heap of open books, with pad and paper in hand and two cups of coffee, and even though she had tried to look at him without being seen, Daniel called to her, 'Come here, don't go, want a coffee? I bought this one for you,' and she sat down next to him, feeling sweet-talked and stupid, but she ended up staying for more than an hour, listening to his stories. At a certain point, she wanted to ask him what was behind those abrupt shifts from disquiet to exaltation, from silence to awkwardness, which fractured Daniel's sense of time and made him look like a ventriloquist's doll that plays a roll chosen ad libitum by an invisible master, and even though she didn't ask, Daniel seemed to read her mind and said, 'Usually it seems to me that people think I live on the moon, that I know nothing about what's going on around me, that my world is limited, or rather, that it's gone off course and is tangled up in the crazy things I discover in books, things I discuss in my articles, things I collect in my house or in the bookshop. This is only partially true, you know. I admit that I've got a passion for history, philosophy, literature . . . which is why it pains me to think that I ignore almost everything with regard to so many moments from the past, and I fight this feeling daily, burying myself in papers and every so often sinking into some idea, oftentimes so far away from any of those things people call "real life" that everyone gets the impression that I'm some aimless wanderer lost in the stacks at the Library of Babel. But that's not the case. It's not that I refuse to look at the world around me, but that I refuse to pretend it's any more important than everything else, you know what I mean? The moments from the past or from the future, the unreal scenes from tales, dreams, the projects we push aside each day that exist in the doubt we stop having in order to live—they're all worlds as true as this one, and I neither abandon nor degrade them. So, I suppose that if I live in so many spaces at once, being absent from this one from time to time should be excusable, don't you think?'"

With a high-pitched voice that turned to dust when it left his lips, Mireaux went on, "Juliana had never heard Daniel talk about himself, and suddenly, to her own dismay, defeated by the spectacular sympathy of our friend, she was seduced by Daniel's words, and she dove into them headlong as if she had immersed herself in a novel. 'I'm going to tell you how I see myself,' Daniel said to her, 'or at least, how I'd like to see myself, as someone who has many bodies simultaneously, all joined together by a very complex nexus of joints that at once touch just as many parallel worlds at an infinite number of points. The function of these Siamese bodies would be to make contact with everything else, to unite with everything, to encompass everything, and for this, I'd have to train these bodies, so that they could learn to sharpen their senses, to rehearse the ways in which their joints must move, their limbs must bend, their abdomens must straighten, in order to achieve a length that would allow them to reach anywhere. And when I say "body," I really mean spirit—one's spirit must reach everywhere. Doesn't that make sense?' Daniel asked. 'Well, not really,' Juliana replied. 'Fine. Let me give you an example. I bet you've never heard of Ehlers-Danlos Syndrome, have you?'"

When Mireaux reached that point, a sudden sadness invaded me: Ehlers-Danlos Syndrome was the illness that had befallen Sofía, the disease that had forced her into seclusion to live out the few years of her life which might otherwise have been normal. Daniel, who never spoke about his sister, as I've said, picked up the topic of that illness quite frequently. In brief, this is how Daniel had explained it to me: "Ehlers-Danlos Syndrome has always been around, but it's only had a name since 1908, when two doctors, the Dane Edvard Ehlers and the Frenchman Henri-Alexandre Danlos—brought together at the Society of Syphilology and Dermatology of Paris by the misfortune of each having fathered a deformed child—decided to investigate the causes of those birth defects and arrived at a carefully crafted classification. Those who suffer from Ehlers-Danlos Syndrome have elastic and spongy skin. They can stretch it with their fingers until visibly separating it from the muscles, sometimes, up to a distance of twelve to sixteen inches. A victim of this disease can pull the skin on his forearm until it turns flabby and hangs from the body, and he can do the same with the skin of his abdomen and his shoulders, until it looks as if he were wearing a rain poncho of human flesh that at any time could be slipped over his head and rolled up neatly in a bag. Their joints are likewise malleable, like the little bones of a fetus, which is why they can bend their knees, elbows, ankles, or necks in ways that are impossible for the rest of us, as if everything in their body were double-jointed or were to break apart with each movement only to come back together just seconds later via rather inhuman movements. For sure, this is what happens more often than not. This is how Hippocrates of Cos, in the fifth century B.C., described the peculiar skin and flaccid joints of the Getai warriors of Thrace, and those of the Scythians and other nomads who roamed along the Danube and the Don. He and his contemporaries thought they had the power to turn into water or smoke, into bubbles or vapor, to infiltrate the houses of their enemies or to refrain from breathing or drinking (and to thereby possess their enemies). It was a superstitious invention, of course, but, as always, it was based on a profound intuition—that absolute elasticity is a feature of either God or the Devil." Daniel liked to finish that explanation, adding or removing a few nuances, with the same question that he always asked half-jokingly: "Don't we speak of elasticity when we say that God is everywhere?"

" 'So Juliana,' Mireaux said Daniel had added that time, 'what I have is a variant of Ehlers-Danlos that doesn't affect my skin or my bones, but rather my imagination.' 'So you mean to say that mentally you're a monster?' she asked him, with a flirting but cautious expression, sipping coffee from her cup, and Daniel responded, 'Perhaps I am. The thing is that it's all the same, since we're all monsters, in one way or another; it's just a matter of delving into one's own birth defects—and still, the more monstrous one is, the greater one's uniqueness.' He lowered his voice, drawing close to Juliana. 'And if being different really upsets you, that's not a problem either. It's a matter of discovering how that deformity can become an extraordinary ability. You know who Niccolò Paganini is, don't you? Long before becoming the greatest violinist in the world, Paganini was the cause of much grief and repulsion in Genoese neighborhoods due to the softness of his body; he was incapable, as a boy, of standing up straight for very long or of pressing against a surface without beginning to gradually take on the shape of that object. During his life, the man had tuberculosis and a grave case of osteomyelitis in his mandible, which at some point left a bone exposed in his jaw, and he had hemorrhoids and urinary infections, and later on syphilis, and the mercury pipettes that he was prescribed to treat it gave his skin the texture of a slightly rotten mango and a dark purple tone, cracked with sores, especially on his face. A moderate diabetes, the mildest of his maladies, had weakened the cornea and rectus muscles behind his eyes, so that, during the culminating movements of his concerts, with his protean will that man would jerk around spasmodically on the stage, reeking of ointment and producing incomparable sounds that no one had heard or dreamed of before, he'd close his eyes and let them roll back slowly in his sockets, and when he opened them back up they were two white balls. People didn't know if they should run to escape or applaud those melodies that seemed to come from an infernal creature. Of course, he didn't earn his talent through a pact made with the Devil, as the public imagined (and as the violinist liked to insinuate). Paganini was another victim of Ehlers-Danlos Syndrome, and he could've ended up like Danlos's son, Victor, transformed into a circus freak, or like Ehlers's son, Alexis, hanged from a rafter of a brothel in Bordeaux, yet he managed to find a parallel world in which his deformed, gaunt body was not only apt, but insuperable. With a violin pressed against his cheek, Paganini, due to the gummy twisting of his knuckles, the freedom of those fingers that had no tendons, was capable of achieving unheard-of notes and chords, and through music he was able to literally reach places in the universe where no human being had ever ventured.'

"'And is that what you intend to do?' intimated Juliana, mischievously entertained, and he had said to her, 'Maybe, but not like that.' 'Ah, no? Then how?' she replied. 'Well, I don't know,' he said, 'and this is my greatest problem, but I think I'll resolve it someday.' 'Come on, no clues?' 'Well, I think there's one. Like all patients who suffer this syndrome, I must force myself to search the air, sea, and land for an object that's a perfect fit for my deformities, in order to convert it into my key that'll unlock another world.' 'You must mean other *worlds* . . .' 'Exactly!' he exclaimed. 'It sounds gloomy,' she said, and Daniel stayed silent for a while and then invited her on a walk through those streets and through one of the few remaining green spaces, just a few blocks away, walled in between the sick patina of the buildings. He began to teach her the scientific names of the trees and flowers, habitats of birds and insects, and over time, those walks transformed into a shared ritual."

Out of all of Daniel's friends, Mireaux had come the closest to sharing that tense romance of thrust and parried words, and his stories consisted of versions of the versions that Juliana had told him, stories that, on her lips, I thought, might have become schematic and monotone but that, coming from the old man's mouth, recovered or acquired a novelistic aftertaste. I told him that I had never understood Juliana and Daniel's relationship. She seemed simple, smooth, seamless, the kind of person who abhors contradiction and trembles in the face of exceptions, and Daniel was, as we knew, contradictory and exceptional. Mireaux laughed for the first time that afternoon, and he said, in his weak and high-pitched voice, "I remember a time, we were at Juliana's house, and Daniel suddenly recalled one of those stories of his that seemed to give way to an encyclopedia of esotericism, and even though it was completely off topic, he began to tell it. Something about a Colombian blacksmith who only manufactured shoes for the left foot, and who received an order to make boots for the soldiers of a battalion that was departing for battle inland, and said, 'Why should I make them if I already have them here?' And at that moment of the story the telephone rang and Daniel got up to answer it, and we were all waiting and wanting to hear the end. And then Adela—do you remember Adela, Juliana's maid? She looked at our disappointed faces and told us not to worry, the end is easy. 'That night, the soldiers, shoeless in the encampment, standing in single file, march down a narrow dirt path, and six feet away from them a missile falls from the sky, and when the fire and smoke dissipate, those who are not dead or torn in two have lost their right legs, and on the following afternoon the blacksmith arrives to deliver the left boots from his warehouse.' And Adela said this and walked out, without any sign of shyness or doubt about the veracity of her tale, and when Daniel returned he told the end of the story, and it was the same, word for word. Then we all kept silent and only Juliana cracked a smile and gave in to expressions of incredulousness and surprise, and she said, 'That Daniel, I don't know where he gets his stories.' It's true that Juliana always had the need to put an end to any inkling of strangeness in her life, to avert her gaze, to refuse to see the surprise, but this, Gustavo, could have led her to be surprising herself. Do you know what I mean? Perhaps on the inside Daniel is simpler than we think," continued Mireaux, "and perhaps Juliana was more complex than you've presumed. I for one, who knew her quite well, can testify that there was much more to that poor girl than meets the eye. Juliana, to put it this way, was two different women, and if you really wish to decode the enigma of why Daniel murdered her, you must start by discovering the other."

TEN

Eight days ago, Daniel noticed that the circle was beginning to break apart, forming two distinct half-moons, each rotating around a central figure: on the left, there was an old man with a seraphic face and scaly temples, his gaze dancing on the surface of a bench, his lips slightly parted; and on the right, a woman about forty years old, her nose dripping, a broken branch between her fingers.

"I read as I always did," said Daniel, "like the high priest of the ogres, and I paused to study the reaction of my audience, their anguished looks; the woman began to bang a wooden, flesh-colored box with the stick, as if it were a primordial instrument and she were the witch of an anachronistic tribe. I immediately resumed the reading, but, out of the corner of my eye, I sensed changes in their attitudes, expressions I hadn't seen before, and I was sure of one thing, *cross-cut incisions, vivisection manuals,* some of the patients were staring at the old man and others at the woman, and they responded to my reading following the orders that these two, with a gesture or a wink, imparted on the rest. The man with a seraphic face and the woman with a dripping nose undoubtedly were spearheading a collective attempt to drive me once again to madness."

These two (who were they?) had issued, Daniel was sure, the order to elicit an outcry through the cyclical repetition of a single act: the constant intonation, in a high and shrill voice, of a chorus of phrases cruelly extracted from his memory. Each time the circle dissolved, the voices would return: *This is what I've come for? What kind of hell have I reached?* And Daniel had set out to capture the speakers red-handed, to identify who it was that had listened to him, first with devotion, then with irony, and now, each and every night, shielded behind this or that rock, curled up under this or that multicolored blanket, was trying to deliver him back to dementia.

"One afternoon I entered the doctor's office, as I did every week, since I was obligated to have a blood test, and I carried a urine sample in a green jar, *stuck inside the waistband of my pants.* There was no one in the office—the nurse wasn't there, must have been in the break-room—but I heard a nervous shriek, like a fingernail scratching a chalkboard, and I went to the back of the room, pulled aside the curtain that was separating the cots from the rest of the office, and found Huk, her face undaunted and slightly tense, *as if it were fixed to her skull with three hairpins,* flanked by the old man with a seraphic face on the left, and on the right the woman with a dripping nose. I heard or thought (at this point it didn't matter), *I saw them bury the bones at the gates of Hell.* The three of them were standing, side by side, their lips pursed, eyes closed, clenching their hands to fists, and I heard a single voice with utter clarity, *The first two cuts will open the back of her neck.*"

The next two days extended the nightmare. The nurses had fled, out of guilt or terror, each time that Daniel, *the profile of a man dressed as a raven,* went near them; their voices, on the other hand, had always been close, too close. Daniel heard them take off in the wind, blowing in the wrong direction, *he heard the metallic clanging of certain objects,* first in his mind, then with his ears, and finally, the echoes made air out of air and faded away.

"There came a time when the conspirators' words followed me everywhere, reaching every corner of the ward—the doctor's office, the examination rooms; they'd suddenly appear between the bathroom walls, *the sea below*. I once awoke in the blackness of my room—it was midnight, lights out, eyelids sealed tight, flooded with fear and cold—and I listened, *no one must ever speak about the past,* the crystal-clear voice, *the nails digging into the pads of my fingers,* a scream echoed over the rest, and a minute later two nurses injected me with a sedative, tried to tie my arms and legs with the belts fastened to the edge of the bed, *facing the sky,* without uttering a word, *the legendary torture chamber,* I thought, or heard, and felt my hands pushing myself up, making me twirl around the room, groping my body, a defenseless puppet, the cadaver of a puppet, and slowly, I drifted off into a dream made of punches and groans, which was no different from my waking state."

In the morning, a doctor visited him, spoke with him for a few minutes, told him it was nothing, an unlit cigarette between his lips. "It's only tension—it accumulates and releases. Go and relax in the courtyard and let out some of that stress."

Daniel followed his orders: went out, took a stroll, confirmed in silence the silence of the place, barely interrupted by a grunt, a bleat, a cackle here and there, which was expected, completely normal, and that night, he even dared to look for a book on the shelves in his room (fewer and fewer were left, he thought, someone was snatching them, one today, another tomorrow, it didn't matter), and he sat for the last time—because this, in effect, was going to be the last time—in the center of the courtyard, to preside over the gradual congregation of his parishioners, and he read them a story.

But during the reading, his neck cranked, his glasses sitting on his nose, "I was sure that things were no longer the same. Huk kneeled down, a few feet from the group, as she never had before, quietly whimpering, and only then could I be sure, she was the only one who understood me, and only a matter of minutes after the meeting began, she stood up, irritated, dragging her blanket on the ground, and disappeared through the hallway entrance. The others watched her walk away, and turned their eyes to me, and then the man with the seraphic face, the woman with the dripping nose, and one of them, I didn't know who, said, 'What do you see in that girl? Why do you follow her around day and night?' And I immediately suspected Huk was in danger."

An hour later the reading ended and the circle slowly dissolved; huddles of madmen were still lingering, but their incoherent phrases incrementally fizzled out. And before eight o'clock, all the doors were closed, lights turned off, a group of nurses vanished behind the door of the examination room, closed by a hinged metal arm, and Daniel showed his head once again, attentive to every noise, awaiting the avalanche of voices which, that night, so he says, strangely never arrived. He walked morosely toward door number one, Huk's room, cupped his hand around his ear and pressed it against the door, lowering his eyebrows, angling his cheekbones upward, as if that movement would enhance his hearing, his skinny hand gripping the handle of the door, and he did all he could to listen, but no sound came from inside.

The Antiquarian reads: An elderly man lies down in his bed to slumber and, to his surprise, awakens in a cubical container of straw and wood, three feet in length on each side, four and a half in height. It is dark inside, and there is a tiny hole in each wall, one of which affords a view into a military encampment, toward a meadow with patches of grass and arid soil. The elderly personage looks through the hole without recognizing anyone, but he hears the metallic clanging of certain objects, which brings him to the realization that in the meadow there are hundreds of women and girls, prostrate, facing the sky, their bodies going through an intricate system of pumps and gears, the legendary torture chamber and its rape machine. A voice says, Kill me, why should I live any longer? And then the elderly man falls asleep and awakens four days later in the countryside, his feet sunken into the lakeshore, a large gray fish flitting between them. So he spends the day fishing and wondering how he got there. And hours later he falls back asleep, only to awaken again in the same cubical container as before, enclosed by the military encampment, but this time he discovers a flashlight inside and directs its cone of sepia light toward the meadow, where he identifies a portion of the machinery, a metallic chain studded with miniature steel bolts and pulleys that creak as they turn, and at the end of a conveyor belt, he sees the trembling body of one woman, one among the many, and sees the face of one killer, one among the many, and he recognizes that face as his own.

ELEVEN

"There's a street downtown that stretches a single block, la Calle Tres Espadas."

"I know how to get there with my eyes closed."

"I'd rather you drive with your eyes open."

"You're the boss."

That bookstore named The Circle is located on a charming corner, speckled with ghastly little trees, signs lit by floodlights, garish cafés and bars, at the intersection of a timeless narrow street and a boulevard lined by cracking sidewalks filled with pigeons, puny sparrows, and paltry gulls that announce the proximity of the sea, which serves as a cemetery for dead fish and as the dump for the city's refuse. It has a narrow first floor, with a group of tables at the back, where customers help themselves to tea and cigarettes and where they open copies of books whose titles may grant them a prestigious air in front of the other patrons. There they converse about topics like the life of a medieval monk invented by the young Thomas Chatterton or the fantastic oeuvre of the fake Ossian.

Even before the store was called The Circle, when Daniel and the others had nothing to do with the business, it had served as the stage for my first dates with a woman who for a short time would be my wife, and that choice had not been mine, but hers, for she had something of that exhibitionist impulse which drives so many people into that crammed hermetic quadrilateral with its tunnel-like stairway rising from the center and leading to the second floor—a collection even more enigmatic and coveted than the first, because it is reserved for only the select few. For three years now, I have scrupulously avoided that place, not so much in order to escape my own memories, though it was that in part, but because I was afraid of finding Daniel's partners or his mother in the vicinity of the bookstore, and of one of them discovering that I had abandoned my friend ever since that night when his nerves had reached their limit and he'd snapped—the night he'd killed Juliana.

After leaving the university, Daniel had completely integrated into the detective-comedic farce of his antiquarian friends. Thanks to a chain of unprecedented acquisitions, he had distinguished himself from the rest as the proprietor of the boldest collection in that dense forest of miracle-hunters. It was during a few months that he spent at Berkeley, taking a course on the preservation of ancient documents, the only break in our friendship, that my wife's illness came on. The cancer was reducing her bones in such a way that they were soon unable to support her weight, and the X rays began to show that within her adult body, to everyone's dismay, her fragmentary skeleton had become a girl's, broken to pieces and unprotected—the little girl that she had once been, she had once again become—from the inside out, until one day she died. When Daniel returned, he arrived with the idea of purchasing the bookstore and turning it into what it is today: that colonial bastion that brings together meticulous researchers, students blessed with apoplectic intelligence, and fishermen trolling for fetishes.

Only after his phone call, my visit to Mireaux, and our conversations at the hospital, which I still haven't finished recounting, did I dare go to that place again, where I ran into Juan Gálvez, another one of Daniel's partners, in the corner of the bookstore, his left hand gripping an instrument that only in The Circle can seem normal—a copper-bladed dagger with a handle made out of a rolled-up scroll, like a small janbiya that one imagines only in the hands of an assassin from *One Thousand and One Nights,* which the old retired attorney was using to cut the packaging tape of a cardboard box that was sure to be filled with books.

Gálvez's daughter and an enormous brown and black owl with glass eyes, nailed to the top of an armoire, with the same greedy smirks on their remarkably similar beaks, kept our company that morning while perching in wait for the arrival of a certain cus-tomer. The man was not surprised to see me. When he spoke, it was as if we had left off the same conversation the previous afternoon, and while I devised the most cautious stratagem to get him to talk about Daniel, with surgical precision he started putting a collection of deadpan anecdotes on the table, as though they were birds that he was about to pierce with the pins of an amateur taxidermist, which had nothing to do, or so it seemed, with the reason for my visit.

"Take Daniel Defoe for example," said Gálvez, "he didn't have ears; his skull was smooth, spherical, and pointed as an ostrich egg, without any other disturbance than his nose and the lower lip of an animal. Did you know that? I bet you didn't. Underneath his wig, Defoe resembled a fish. But if you read his books you won't find a woman whose beauty doesn't begin and end with a pair of supernaturally perfect ears, a prologue and epilogue of absolute beauty. Nicolai Gogol, on the other hand, erred on the side of excess, with his monstrous, elliptical, drooping nose, so big that the tip would fit between his lips, in such a way that at night Gogol awoke suckling his own proboscis, as if he had returned to the elephantine arms of his Ukrainian wet nurse. In one of his tales, that nose is the protagonist—it comes off a face and goes for a walk through the streets as though nothing were out of the ordinary. The Romantics suffered that kind of curse. One need not go further than Byron, who was the victim of a spastic paraplegia that wrenched his foot during childhood, making it look like the blunt, forked hoof of a nandu, which is why he used to make love with his boots on or with a linen sheet wrapped around his leg from his calf to the tip of his toe. And in that creative response he was contrary to Gogol and to Defoe—in his books, the characters seem to exist only from the waist up. The former corrected the world, the latter severed it, do you see? The case of Toulouse-Lautrec was different. He used to hide from the world's gaze his ridiculously tiny legs and big pumpkin head, but he would exhibit them as substitutes for his microscopic phallus when he locked himself in the bordellos of Paris, among prostitutes, cardsharps, and opium smokers eaten away by syphilis, and he never refrained from displaying them in his artwork. Whether confined within his merry inferno or extolled in his painting, his deformities held a different meaning, acquired a meaning that was, let's say, the recognition of monstrosity. When all is said and done, all artists are monsters.

"That's the same thing Daniel thought," added Gálvez, "because I bet you wish to speak about Daniel, right? Well, Daniel, as you know, has always had an obsession for differences, the need to discover the ways in which a being that's distinct from the others can modify the world or adapt it to him in order to keep living, or decide to cut himself off and destroy himself as an escape. It's not hard to imagine that this obsession comes from Sofía's misfortune, his poor little sister, whom, I think, you did get to know, but it's also related, and very much so, to that tendency of Daniel's to think about himself as some kind of freak. The fact of the matter is that the idea of annihilation as an escape, the most radical exit, is the only one in which Daniel had complete faith, and that's been his guiding light and his downfall.

"For him, books are the registries of vexation, the testimony of men's anxiety to transform or annihilate everything in order to start anew, but what we're dealing with here is a contradictory anxiety, because books too are responsible for maintaining tradition and continuity. That's why Daniel appreciates the most outlandish works. If he is fond of any tradition, it's that of over-indulgence and disturbance. And in turn, when he rereads them, he becomes an inhabitant in a Quixotesque hallucination, where nothing is what it seems, a series of distortions, errors, paranoid coincidences that his mind perceives as lucidity.

"You know that after the continuous sedation they subjected him to in the hospital, he lost his ability to speak for a while, right? What you don't know, I bet, is that when his mother took him those first books and he started to escape that deaf-mute marasmus into which he had run, or so he says, even though he attentively looked them over, if someone asked him what he was reading, no matter what book he had in hand, he could only repeat a single story, always the same one, which surprisingly was not among the books that he had in his room.

"'In the Chinese province of Jiangsu,' Daniel would say, 'there's a town called Changzhou, where a boy was born and named Feng Menglong toward the end of the sixteenth century. Barely a young man, Feng Menglong became a traveling poet and writer of fantastic tales that he published in 1620 under the title *Yushi Mingyan*, that is, *Illustrious Words to Instruct the World*. In 1638, he had a child with a fussy, insolent vagabond, and they lived together until, one day in 1640, after confirming that their child was crippled and would never surpass sixteen inches in height, Feng Menglong killed his wife with a blade used to slaughter rams and left her curled up, resting against a tree at the intersection of two roads in the outskirts of Changzhou, so that the ravens would devour her.

Driven by the fate of his son, Feng Menglong built in his house a rectangular room with bamboo corners, reinforced with chestnut, and walls made of ash and eucalyptus planks, and there he shut away the boy. Twice a year he put his son to sleep with a drink he purchased at the neighboring village, in order to use the night for tearing down the room and rebuilding it, subtracting half a foot in height from each wall, each baseboard, each edge of the ceiling, so that when the boy awoke the following morning, he'd feel that he had grown an astonishing half-foot over the course of a single night. Since he himself was the only point of reference capable of giving away the story, Feng Menglong forbade his son from seeing him, and kept him a prisoner in that room without any doors or windows or orifices other than those through which his meals were served to him twice daily, with access to the septic well, where he'd urinate and defecate and which the father would clean only when each remodeling project was carried out. When Feng Menglong died, no one in Jiangsu suspected the existence of that son, whom everyone believed to have disappeared along with his mother; the child remained cloistered in that personal world his father had constructed for him, which at the time was barely an isomorphous cube measuring nineteen inches on each side, and months later it became the coffin in which they carried him off for burial.'

"It's strange," said Gálvez, shooting a remorseful glance toward the desk, where his daughter and the stuffed owl seemed to form an escutcheon of misanthropy. "When Daniel was telling that story, he sounded like a robot, without recognizing the content of his own words. But the story summarizes the unnatural link that joined Daniel to Juliana, do you see? Daniel was that father willing to reconstruct the world to please his child, and what's worse is that, between them, the element that Daniel perceived as a threat

was himself. He was like a caged monster that, by bashing the bars
in defiance, was to shatter the fantasy that both of them had lived
for just shy of a year, which is to say, the illusion that they were a
regular couple. Not happy, no, not that, but regular. Juliana was
a sleepy, unworried woman, and she never understood that her
relationship with Daniel was unsustainable. For what was she? A
painter without much of an imagination, a newspaper illustrator,
a schoolteacher, a daughter from a family of provincial merchants,
raised in the mediocrity of a city without contact to the outside
world, an unblemished girl, satisfied and aware of it. She would fill
halfway with joy over most things and had forgone any sudden burst
of creativity in order to seek out an ordinary life, a routine. Her
only thirst for adventure was for finding a formulaic, appeasing way
to manage each aspect of her life, and her greatest expression of
strength was to do everything possible to distinguish herself from
her servants. Do you recall when Daniel hired a maid whose name,
it turns out, was also Juliana, and so Juliana decided to change that
girl's name, to rechristen her Adela, terrified at having anything
in common with the poor girl? Do you? I still remember Adela,"
continued Gálvez. "A fine-looking girl—I wonder what's become
of her. You had to call her three times before she realized she was
being addressed by that arbitrary name. Do you remember her?"
he asked again.

"Of course I do," I said, and it was the truth. Hard to forget
that maid who laughed heartily and shook hands with guests
as fluidly as a femme fatale, as if she were always on the brink
of taking them out on the dance floor, her cunning eyes, her
vampiric teeth, her lips, always painted with inflammatory
colors. I took advantage of the opportunity to ask Gálvez about
the last thing Mireaux had said to me, the thing that had dis-
concerted me so.

"Mireaux says," I told Gálvez, "that Juliana was much more complex than the impression everyone had of her, that two women were locked inside her."

"Well," said Gálvez, "I don't have the foggiest idea what Sebastian means by that. Juliana was flat as a tortilla—she sought security, and on occasion leapt into a world even more complacent and mild than her own. Because she was, as you know, from a family that had come to the city to escape the war, she was not one of the miserable peasants who arrived with all their belongings on their backs, but hers was one of those middle-class families from the provinces, who were lords in the land they hailed from, and here became no one and dissolved into this amnesiac crowd of immigrant, anonymous, unimportant ghosts. I think that for this reason her expectation was for absolute peace. In Juliana's presence, Daniel had to control himself (even with suffocation) in order to hide his true character, that carnivalesque overflow of imagination and torsion, the peremptory urge to see things through every deformed crystal that he could find. He decided to put forth the effort, but then she would have to adapt to the game. The day that Juliana failed, that entire world crashed down, and the paradise built by Daniel, as in Feng Menglong's story, became a coffin."

TWELVE

"And in the morning," Daniel continued, "one of the nurses found Huk, sitting on her bed in room number one, her legs folded up against her belly, her arms wrapped in front, her hands curled around her shins, her fingers twisted together, fingernails broken, fingertips torn off, feet side by side, face turned away, neck swollen, open mouth and eyes, black hair loose on her shoulders, a ball of blood in her left eye, a long, bright incision covering her breasts and forming a series of erratic lines that went down toward her pelvis. A couple of flies crawled on her forehead, crusty strings hung from each eyelid, her teeth broken, the corner of her mouth slit open, snipped with a pair of scissors that still rested on the pillow, her cheeks bloated; the woman, almost a girl, was dead in the same position in which she spent her days, sitting in the hallway, and under her, a multicolor blanket was laid out upon the comforter, folded in half to form a triangle."

The nurse, a young man, barely older than Huk, had stumbled into the hallway trembling, his eyes rolling back in his head, forgetting to close the door behind him. And Daniel had been the first to step inside the room (drawn there, he later told the police, by a scream which the nurse claimed to have never let out), only to leave immediately, convulsing in disgust and grief, and bumping into the old man with the seraphic face and the woman with a dripping nose, who came running down the hall, falling flat on his face, amidst a swarm of morbid, jocular assistants and patients, their irritating laughter, the sane and insane with the same expression of fear and pleasure. And Daniel stayed there for about two hours, watching the parade of outsiders enter and exit the premises, some in black, some in white, *wandering migrant masses,* he had heard, that flooded the hallway, with briefcases, notebooks, a stretcher that was brought in empty and taken out with a long, thin object on it, Huk's body, wrapped up, *night was falling, and a caretaker was covering it with a veil,* he had heard, or had thought, the green sheet stained with blood. They took her away forever.

"That evening," Daniel said, "two nurses prohibited my mother from entering the hospital, asked her to return the following day. 'Why, what's wrong?' she asked. 'Nothing, come back later.' And they took me to the office in the basement and kept me there with a skull on top of a pile of papers, the narrow and tall windows, with bars around them, at the height of the sidewalk outside. Many hours passed, and finally two policemen dressed in street clothes, a skinny one and a fat one—the first with canker sores on his lips, and the second with patches of psoriasis on the back of his hands and the edge of his eyebrows—came to speak with me.

"A medical technician, responsible for the autopsy, had opened up Huk's body and discovered a sticky, half-decomposed mess, soft in parts, brittle in others, that filled her whole digestive tract, spherical and compacted handfuls of a substance now solid, now spongy, soggy in her stomach, liquid in her pancreas, and in her colon, syrupy, yellowish, and indecipherable. After extending his incision upward, in the esophagus, behind Huk's dark, smooth skin, the poor woman, almost a girl, the doctor had found more balls of that material, these ones almost dry and uncorrupted, unscathed by digestion. It was paper, dozens of sheets, hundreds, thousands of pieces of paper, some cloth spines, some bookmarks, they were the pages of many books, sprawling volumes, yanked out by the dozen, wrinkled, crumbled, and behind them, when the contrite, malevolent doctor had plunged his scalpel farther into the skin of her throat, more pieces of paper meticulously folded, *elephant folios, imperial quartos, bound with paper, parchment and Valencian calf,*" Daniel had thought, or heard, in the end it was the same.

One of the policemen, the one with the discolored hands, had described the rest of the scene, with hatred and joy. "'The doctor used his tweezers,' Daniel explained, 'later the tips of knives and scalpels, and had finished sinking his gloved hands into her, his pinky entering her gall bladder, more paper, an object, a sheaf of liquefied pages, scraps that had begun to dissolve, and in her mouth, the forensic specialist found a large sheet of printed paper folded in half, the only one left intact.'" *It must have seemed to him,* Daniel had thought, or heard, *like a document filed away forever in a warm, circular bookcase.*

"What the paper said, if it said anything, which details were certain, which ones inventions in the psoriatic's mind, I don't know," Daniel said, "but the questions came immediately. The skinny policeman spoke with a smirk on his ulcerous lips, his mouth but an open sore beneath his nostrils. 'It's your second time,' he said, his legs crossed, tapping his fingers on the sole of his shoe to the rhythm of a military march. *Two unknown armies waged war in the outskirts,* I heard," said Daniel, "or that's what I thought, and then the psoriatic's voice, and the voice of the man with ulcers, released an unstoppable sequence of questions: 'Were you the only one close to Huk? What kind of relationship did you have? How many times did you attack her?'

"He drew his face close to mine, his voice floating in the air: 'What threats did you use to convince her? Why did you torture her?' His questions fluttered up and down through the office, white words inside black words, that's what they felt like, a thread of light with a halo of darkness around them."

"Why did you do it?" Daniel heard, and within that phrase he heard another one, like a beam of light in the dark sleeve of a tunnel. "Moist in the stomach, liquid in the pancreas."

"I was the only murderer in the ward, everyone saw me following the girl around, all day long, week after week, the nurses witnessed the constant panic in the poor girl's eyes, oh, how terror paralyzed her each time I came up to her, she'd collapse on the ground wherever she was and would whimper, and I, they said, though it's untrue, tormented her hour after hour by reading her cruel passages from books that I kept on the shelves in my room, what stories had I told her, what had I forced on her, and according to the police, the doctor and the nurse who led the conversations in the courtyard had attested to my rebelliousness, my perpetual refusal to converse, the way I always responded to questions with fragments from books, the way that I obliged the other patients to speak about the things that disturbed them, worried them, happened to them, how I sabotaged the operation of the therapy circle that the doctor with a seraphic face and nurse with the runny nose conducted on the ground of the central courtyard, each and every afternoon, and what did I have to say about this.

" 'Are you going to pretend you're crazy again?' said the psoriatic cop. 'How much longer?' And the one with the canker sores on his lips laughed, 'A shame about that girl.' How had I deceived her to get her to open the door for me, what kind of lies did I tell her to get her to let me into her room, what must she have felt when I made her open her mouth, how did I put the papers into her body, how many hours did she take to die, how far in did I have to stick my hand, why hadn't the poor girl bitten me, snapped clean those fingers that were killing her, at what moment in the night had she given up, what had I seen in her eyes while I choked her, why had I left the scissors on the bed, how many books had I used and where were the other ones? At first, it was the voice of the psoriatic, then the one with canker sores, then there were many other voices."

Every evening, after the first meeting, the Antiquarian emerges from his reams of paper to take to the spiraling street, a book in front of his eyes, hidden from the passersby and the beggars who cram into the city's increasingly crowded sidewalks, and he walks until coming face-to-face with the door to the house or motel, the plastic geraniums or the murmur of people, and the same woman in the window, her fingernails red, her eyes tiny as bullet holes (or a scalpel's incisions), her arms pale, she says to him, My name is Juliana, what's yours? And he tries to remember, doubts, runs for cover in his house, crouching down in the center of his library, his books laid out and open, some on top of others, forming columns five feet high, placed in a circle around him, like birds of prey that might swoop down and devour him.

THIRTEEN

"Don't you get tired of going in circles around this city?"

"Ha! That's a strange question."

"Strange?"

"I don't know anyone in the world who does anything else."

The house of Fernando Pastor is a rickety wooden box on the second floor of a building on a cul-de-sac. In his front yard cats and dogs walk back and forth, and two armies of barefoot children run around playing with plastic rifles and guns, or curling their fingers into revolvers while dodging puddles of oil and potholes in the concrete that bulges from the heat and humidity, as though it were reaching for the low-hanging branches of withering rubber trees that crouch in line down the sidewalk. Pastor is an unusual ex-naval officer who never served on a ship and who, due to a slight lesion in his eyes during his early years in the service, coupled with his uncanny interest in books and history, had been assigned to a sedentary, mind-numbing position as the administrator of a small naval museum, a short walk from the wharf, where he would often go at lunchtime to contemplate the bustle of people arriving at that destination, on journeys he had once desired for himself. In the museum, amid scale models of beached ships, bullet-spattered uniforms that still lay dying, broken swords, surrendered flags, and old binnacle logs left open for eternity to the page referencing the sinking, Pastor had sheltered himself for twelve static years, while the rest of the country was the scene of a war that surpassed—in confusion and cruelty—any of the moments trapped in the urns, coffers, and bells of glass and plastic that surrounded him, until one morning when he received a memo that summoned him to the airport at the naval base on a not too distant date whereupon he would have to embark on a mission to the Red Zone.

For three consecutive nights he thought about it and finally decided to request a discharge, but the Navy tried him for defection and kept him in prison for six months before they let him go. Then, he had to resort to the contacts he had made over the years at the museum, and he soon started to purchase and sell antiques, entering a network that is so exclusive and so coveted that in little time he had made friends or enemies with everyone in that industry, and before he knew it he had become a minority shareholder of The Circle.

In the living room of his home, which might as well have been an extension on the museum, a stream of dying light magnetized the air inside, and with it, a cloud of mosquitoes that flew, a few seconds there and a few seconds back, and stopped on the molding of a moistened, carious pilaster that appeared to have been pilfered from some seaside fortress and placed at random in the middle of the room.

The first time I saw Daniel and Juliana together was here, some four or so years back. He was sunken into his own shoulders, as if silenced by force. She was wearing that artificial smile of hers to feign normality. Daniel's left forefinger was loosely placed between Juliana's thumb and middle finger, a precarious contact that seemed to have no other purpose than to make them both feel that neither was free.

Pastor remembered that night and many others like it, in this house or at Daniel's, or at Juliana's, where Adela, the maid, more and more often seemed like the only carefree and light-spirited creature, surrounded by the living dead.

" 'They've robbed me of my name, but they won't rob me of my happiness,' Adela would always sing when Juliana and Daniel were not around."

And Pastor also remembered the evening, almost a year later, when Daniel had been in this room, his hair stuck to the forehead of his sweaty skull, his hands and eyes darkened to a cloudy violet, his cheeks, nostrils, and lips waxed by perspiration and tears, booze on his breath, completely hammered, saying that he had committed an atrocity and no one was going to forgive him.

"Five minutes before Daniel arrived," Pastor said with his dark liquid voice, "Juliana had called on the phone. With the tone of a weeping girl, she said to me, 'Fernando, Daniel is probably headed to your place, he's acting like a madman, he's been drinking and is out of his mind, and he keeps repeating nonsense. You know that he never touches liquor, right? I don't know what got into him. I came home,' Juliana continued, 'and he was here, drunk, sitting on the bathroom floor, the medicine cabinet open, pills scattered everywhere—a complete wreck. Daniel, poor Daniel, babbling, and he just up and left, fell down the stairway and ran out on foot—at least on foot and not behind the wheel—and since you, Fernando, live so close, it wouldn't surprise me if he goes to your place. I'm still calling other people, but I don't know what else to do. And on top of it, Adela isn't here, and I have no one to help me.'

"And wouldn't you know it," said Pastor, "Daniel appeared a few minutes later, in a state much worse than she had described, wearing only one shoe, the other sockless foot cut up and blood-stained. He might have been rushing across the avenue between Juliana's house and mine; or he might have run into some barbed wire, or he might have stepped on shards of broken bottles that vagabonds throw near the monument, or he might have been bitten by the dog of some night watchman. Daniel left a trail of red footsteps on the stairway and sat down on this couch, shaking with spasms, like an inconsolable boy unleashing fears and tantrums from his chest, but refusing to come clean about what had happened. It was then," said Pastor, "that Daniel pronounced that horrendous phrase that I will never be able to forget. 'I have killed Juliana,' he said. 'I've just killed her, with a knife,' he said, 'with this knife right here,' and he moved his fist toward me and opened his fingers until his palm was flat, and there was nothing in his hand, Gustavo, but he kept staring deeply at the empty space, as if to say, 'This is the material evidence of my crime.'

"I didn't know what to do," said Pastor. "My first impulse, after a few moments of commotion, since I suppose I was shaking too, was to grab Daniel by the neck and drag him into the bedroom, throw him on the bed, and leave for Juliana's house, but I took only a few steps and thought, This can't be, there's no way, Daniel hasn't killed her, he's hallucinating, I just spoke with her on the phone. Even if Daniel had returned to her house after the call, then attacked her, and had left running all the way here, it would've been impossible to cover that distance in such a short period of time.

"I traced my steps," Pastor went on, extending two fingers in a gesture that cleaved through the room, staging with his eyes that scene from his memory, while the cloud of mosquitoes left the pilaster and swarmed acrobatically around our heads.

"So I decided to call Juliana. The telephone rang several times and the final ring was eclipsed by knocking on my bedroom door, which suddenly opened and closed. Pierced by shock and soaked with booze, sprayed with dozens of specks of blood that were beginning to form a paste on his ankles, like nailed bones, Daniel just stood there in the doorway looking me in the eyes, and at that moment, in the earpiece, I heard Juliana saying, 'Hello? Who's there? Daniel? Fernando?'

"And Daniel kept staring at me, his eyes skewering my eyes, until Juliana's shouts on the phone became frenetic and occupied the entire room. Then Daniel said to me, with his hollow and serene voice, in his only instant of apparent calm that night: 'Don't believe her, she's a ghost.'

"For quite a while after that," Pastor said, "Daniel had me listening to his delirium, plunging into bursts of rage or grief, and when he wasn't howling he would describe that impossible crime in many different ways. 'I found her with another guy,' he said, 'and I waited for her in her house,' or 'I followed her on the street,' or 'I found some photos and then saw red.'

"Yet, no matter what the discrepancies, in every version he was admitting that he had killed her with that knife, and was showing me his dirty, empty hands. After a few hours the labyrinth of his drunkenness turned into exhaustion and Daniel fell asleep on my bed," Pastor said.

"On the phone, Juliana suggested I let him rest. 'Tomorrow we'll see if there's some explanation,' she said. So I took her advice, and very early the following day Daniel woke up sore and sick and, so it would seem, with only a distant memory of what had happened. I served him a couple of cups of coffee and something to eat, which he turned down, and after taking a quick shower and putting on a pair of my shoes, he changed his demeanor and, as if in jest, yet sadly, said something about being in someone else's shoes. Then, as was his custom, he started jumping from topic to topic and let his monologue transform into an encyclopedic orgy."

Pastor got up and walked through the room. I followed him to the window that faced the lot on the street corner. The children of both armies were zigzagging, chasing one another, prowling behind one another's backs, without marks or flags or signs to differentiate ally from enemy. They kept jumping, shouting warnings, groaning in pain, or squealing with excitement. And the dogs came up to them with jaws hanging open or ran away howling to take cover between the wheels of a car.

"That morning," Pastor said, "when Daniel appeared to have his strength back and I asked him about the night before, he couldn't say a word, or he didn't take my question seriously. He immediately asked for the phone, which I handed to him, and I heard him make a call. Without letting me inquire further, he excused himself, alleging that he urgently needed to speak with Yanaúma." Pastor looked at me. "You know Yanaúma, right? The old-timer from the Biblio Path."

"Of course," I replied. "Cabecita Negra."

"That's the one. I didn't hear what they spoke about, but perhaps there was nothing to hear. In any case, he must not have been involved in that night's scandal, which was all I was interested in. Daniel said that he was hunting down a certain book and Yanaúma seemed to be on the brink of obtaining a copy. I don't recall the title, but I do remember that Daniel took advantage of the opportunity to lead the conversation astray once again. 'There's a story in that book,' he said, 'that I want to have a look at. It's about a man who's locked in a prison and has only been allowed to take with him a compendium of fantasy stories. The prison time leads him to concoct the senseless notion that those tales contain the key to the man he'll become one day. So the guy reads and rereads the book in search of the information that could reveal to him the secret code of his future, which he interprets as a hope for freedom, and he reads it so many times, with such obstinacy and dedication, that his mind clears of all other ideas, until it turns blank and begins to take on the form of the book, an intelligence made of pages and words, arranged in the order of an imaginary tale in all its grandeur. Then, submerged in that tide of amnesia, the guy thinks that in those pages there's the key to the man he once was and has forgotten, a man who was free in the past. So he concludes that it's his obligation to read that book until the reading enables him to solve the riddle.'

"Daniel had told that story in barely more than one breath and sipped the last drop of his coffee before leaving and saying goodbye without giving any further explanation. Fourteen days later, Juliana was really dead," Pastor said, "and I still don't know if what I saw that night was a sign, or a practice run, or if it was an exorbitant theatrical stratagem that Daniel had staged, perhaps unconsciously, in order to ask for help. Anyway, neither she nor I knew how to interpret what would come to pass later on. I went to visit Juliana that night, and she asked me to forget about the matter, just like that, without saying anything further. She didn't want to touch the topic again."

"And did you see Daniel again before Juliana's death?" I asked Pastor.

"Yes, I saw him one afternoon in the bookstore," he said. "He was unpacking a box. I wanted to know if he got the book that Yanaúma was going to find for him, and Daniel seemed not to know what I was referring to, self-absorbed as he was, opening the seal of the package he had in his hands with a dull knife, the sight of which made me shudder. 'I have no idea what you're talking about,' he said. 'I haven't heard from Yanaúma in weeks.'

Pastor walked me to the street, turning away from the ruckus of the battle erupting in the corner lot. I noticed that he was tense and sad and, to distract him from the topic, it occurred to me to ask him, "How do you think these kids tell which army they each belong to?"

Pastor scrunched his face up and replied, "I used to wonder the same thing, but later I learned that those were the rules of my childhood, not the rules of today. Now, everyone fights to save his own hide."

He said this and from his pocket removed a key to open the gate to the street, and as I stepped through, he added one more thing, pursing his lips as if a tiny insect had just slipped between them and begun to crawl down his tongue. "Did Mireaux tell you about Juliana, that she was two-faced? If he did, knowing that old geezer, it's because there is something else, and only he himself can give you the answer. That's how he is. Your inquiry will not be uncalled for. If I were you, I'd speak with him again."

FOURTEEN

"The police," Daniel continued, "had come every day following Huk's death, had interrogated each nurse, each doctor. It was useless. No one was lingering in the hallways at night. Two orderlies would stay after the doors were closed, past eight o'clock, but no one heard anything, they had said, and then, the psoriatic cop and the one with canker sores had wanted to speak with all the patients, one by one. They sat them down in the office, the skull atop a pile of paper, and they traveled each time toward the edge of gravelly cliffs through the languages of the mad, each one a distinct, unique code governed by no law, individuals who seemed immersed in an infinite battle with their hands, which moved like the blades of a windmill, their heads in perpetual rotation, and a glow in their pupils seeming to announce the arrival of a complete idea, a never-before-crystallized phrase. And the police, convinced from the beginning that I was the culprit, after talking to seven or eight of them, had decided that it was pointless.

"But it's not true, Gustavo," Daniel said, "you know it's not. You're a linguist and have worked with people like them. You can sift through the twists and turns of those undefined phrases, discover the patterns, parse out the avalanche of words that madness forces them to release. You can try to understand what they mean when they open their mouth and obsessive, sickly stanzas gush from someplace in their mind which, for everyone else, including me and the police, mean nothing."

Daniel had gone over the events of that night hundreds of times: the orderlies at the end of the hallway, playing cards perhaps, maybe watching a program on television. A man and a woman (maybe they were lovers, and right then going at it—they were always scheduled for the same shift). The nurses, each in a room, the doors unlocked, almost all of them, forty in total, thirty-eight without counting Huk's and Daniel's. Anyone could have slipped into the hallway, slithered to room number one, the closest to the office, or who knows, if you think about it, walked without any haste. It was not unusual to walk through the hallway—one had to go to the bathroom or stretch out one's legs every once in a while. The rules prohibited it, but no one obeyed them.

"Such are the regulations in this clinic. There are two kinds: those that are not followed and those that serve no purpose, you see?" said Daniel, pointing around with his chin. "They prohibit electrical devices in my room, seal off the sockets, it's risky, something could happen, I can hurt myself or someone else, yet I have an oil lamp, a portable stove with a kerosene bottle full to the top. I could light this place on fire if I wanted to, and the next day there would be nothing left, *recently extinguished pyres, ash and charcoal,* Daniel heard. (And he told me he did.) "At this very instant I've just heard a voice, they're here, but that's beside the point," he said.

Daniel had written down a list of the remaining patients, thirty-eight, and then ruled out the numskulls and space-cases, as well as those who would only repeat one phrase, always the same one, in any circumstance, like Huk, the poor woman, almost a girl. He also erased from his list the dumbstruck, the blind, the deaf, and the crippled, and, so as not to lose time, he removed the old lady who would always eat the same piece of bread, the one who never said anything, and the old man who tied his shoes from morning to night. And finally, he deleted those who were under lock and key in the evenings, and those lost in themselves, and then there were only three names left on his list.

"So would you look at that," Daniel said, "the three of them occupy rooms near Huk's, and they are, don't laugh, reasonable people," he said, and he let out a squawk. "I tell you not to laugh and I laugh, what can I do? It's all so absurd." And then he said, "You can speak with them—strange birds, of course, but peaceful. In the beginning, it's hard to understand why they're here. When you hear them, everything seems to make sense—for a few minutes, until you notice the deceit. Each one is ruled by a personal logic, made to fit the scale of the dimension of that world, a personal island they alone inhabit, without any company. But don't get me wrong, they're not insane, indeed they're not, they recognize what goes on around them, even though they say so in peculiar ways. You know more about this than I do. You'll be able to understand what they tell you; if one of them saw something, knew, heard, or intuited something, you'll have the means to recognize it, if you talk to them. Please, that's why I've called you. You know about these things, it's your job. I'm afraid that, sooner or later, they're going to prohibit me from having contact with others.

"Do it however you want to," Daniel said, "and only if you want to help me. You're going to ask why I've already crossed off my list all the patients from the adjacent ward. There are forty rooms over there, forty people, and that's the wing for the dangerous patients, the patients with histories of violence, almost always sent to the clinic from some prison. But look, Gustavo," he said, "I think I already told you yesterday, there's no way to get from that ward to this one, unless someone cuts through the hallway on that side and crosses the employees' locker room and the gardener's quarters, and then heads straight toward the reception desk, passing by the guards and nurses (and if this were possible, patients would escape daily), and then cuts through the employee cafeteria before crossing the hallway to this wing of the clinic—not to mention that one would have to repeat this entire route on the way back. No one, except for a ghost, can do such a thing without being seen, don't you think? So now, you tell me, please, are you going to help me with this?" he asked, and from his shirt pocket he removed a folded piece of paper with three names and three numbers penciled in the margin.

The Antiquarian reads: A crowd kicks down the door to a dwarf's house: four eucalyptus posts, one beam, miniature furniture. The intruders sniff the premises, bent at the waist, searching beneath the rags and looms, behind the pots, inside the jugs of black water, and they finally find him—a minuscule little man—behind the house, hiding in the latrine. They leave the home dragging the dwarf uphill, and, when he is sure that they have left, his son comes out from under a bed, his eyes wide, his teeth and tongue green, a boy the same size as his father—though perhaps at that moment he too stops growing. The son follows the footsteps of the mob, hollering into the distance, he travels for one day and one night and the trail leads him to a cave. In the darkness he finds a finger, a heel, a nose. He immediately recognizes that these are pieces of his father, and he spends three days collecting them, he arranges them, recomposes the body, and then, propped on a stone at the entrance to the cave, his hands on his knees, the cadaver of the dwarf, mended back together, looks gigantic: thirty necks, sixty eyes, six hundred fingers. The Antiquarian turns the page and continues to the next story.

FIFTEEN

"What's that?"

"Nothing. A traffic light that by design produces gridlock."

"Hmm. I guess that's what laws are for, right?"

Mireaux said, "Do you see this, Gustavo? Do you know what it is?" Standing in the corner of his pentagonal office at the newspaper, the old man had just slid closed the rolltop of a giant piece of wooden furniture that was not a desk from the last century, as I had suspected, or a baby grand piano, but rather a monstrously comic apparatus, made of tin drums, tubes, and crystal bulbs, with handles that turned on both sides, and a transparent glass cover with two metal blades wrapped in fiber jutting out on the edges, and between them something that looked like a submarine viewfinder. Mireaux lifted a knee-high lever, whereupon the tin tubes let out a harsh, raspy groan and, after a momentary tremor, began rotating in opposite directions. A sheet of diagonal light emanated from the middle drum, lighting up the dust in the air and the black silver-plated wings of a moth that took flight from the lamp at that very instant and kept fluttering in and out of the luminous beam. The light bounced back and forth between two rows of concave mirrors stationed above the drum, and Mireaux made haste to cover the wall with a yellowish-cream cloth that he pulled down from the top of a bookcase that had been blocking the fifth window of his office. (The other four were covered.) Then, the sheet of light turned solid and steady against that screen, and its glow started composing a collection of shapes that, bit by bit, grew more and more defined, as if summoned from some other dimension.

"In the beginning, they called this machine a *zoetrope,* and then a *praxinoscope,*" said Mireaux, while images multiplied in his spellbound retinas. "That's why," he continued to say, "in its most primitive version, that it was very small. Later, near the end of the nineteenth century, its inventor, a French painter and mechanic named Émile Reynaud, transformed it into this enormous, grotesque contraption, baptizing it with one contradictory, oneiric name: the Optical Theater of the Luminous Shadows. Thousands of people journeyed through western Europe to see Reynaud's laboratory, arriving with the same stunned excitement as that of children who enter a magician's tent, to witness the moving image of a few laughable gnomes that Reynaud himself had sketched out and colored by hand, dwarfs lying on their backs, balancing balls and cubes with their feet, doing stunts and juggling with their arms behind their backs. The spectators had to wait in line for hours and take turns, because, in the earliest incarnations of the Optical Theater of the Luminous Shadows, the image was only visible through an individual peephole, like the one you see before you. This one, however, as you must have noticed," said Mireaux, proudly pointing at the extravagant instrument, "is capable of projecting its moving figures on a screen. That means it was assembled after 1892. And now look here," he said, turning a crank that neatly rolled up the film of one cartridge, only to place it inside another. "What you're about to see is one of the oldest movies in the world."

A portly man with a bowler hat and a gigantic mustache that split his face in two appeared against the office wall, his face, hands, clothes, grainy, the expression in his eyes bored. A rustic landscape of rudimentary brush strokes extended behind him as the man walked at a slow gait, looking at us with insistence and curiosity, until finally coming to a rest, visible only from the waist up. Suddenly, as if alerted by some signal, he commenced a slapstick choreography made up of tragicomedic expressions and awkward gestures. His eyebrows bopped at the base of his forehead along with a stiff, shiny, plastic hairdo that resembled a piece of polished leather. He moved his lips without producing any sound, while his veins swelled with hysterical shrieks and his entire head swung like a pendulum and rotated without his neck's turning, which made his body look as if it had been built from a single sheet of iron. "His name was Felix Galipaux," Mireaux said at the end of a pause.

"He was an actor, a comedian, popular in the southeast of France and the north of Italy and Spain for certain street routines, always starring this character of his, a mixture of several European rulers, although, most of all, a barely exaggerated version of Umberto I, king of Italy and prince of Piedmont." When Mireaux said this, the man bowed and then jumped a few times, his eyes fixed on a point invisible to us.

"In 1896," continued Mireaux, "due to a military blunder in Abyssinia, Umberto had halted the expansion of his empire, and this defeat, which forced him to embezzle agricultural funds for the war effort, had condemned the poor of Italy to a wonderful famine that killed them off by the thousands. In the towns of the north, in Novara, in Alessandria, and farther east, in Torino, people wanted to stone the monarchy, and in Umberto's absence, they aimed at Galipaux, who found fortune in his ability to rile the masses with these idiotic expressions and his resemblance to the king.

The portly man gazed into an imaginary sky and extended his grimy fingers, and his lips resumed their angry, ill-humored huffing and puffing. It was the beginning of a speech. "For almost

thirty years," Mireaux said, "after the invention of the praxinoscope, Reynaud refused to use photographs as raw material for
his movies. He always went back to drawings and engravings,
convinced that the new medium's value was not in its punctilious
reproduction of the world, but in the deformity that the human
hand could inoculate in the copy. Toward the end of the century,
however, Edison's kinetoscope made Reynaud's Optical Theater
of the Luminous Shadows look like an obsolete, lesser gadget, and
the Frenchman, on the verge of bankruptcy, let his arm be twisted.
It was then that he hired Galipaux and collected in thousands of
rough photographs the routine of this Umberto I impersonator."
Galipaux leaned his head toward the side and let his eyes wander
between mine and Mireaux's.

"But Reynaud," said the old man, passing through the sheet
of light toward the other side of the room, "was not satisfied by
reducing his Optical Theater to the role of a mere copy machine,
and he wished to imbue his characters with a certain complexity
that they did not possess in the shallowness of a flat image thrown
against a wall. The human beings on Edison's films looked like
stains, randomly similar to creatures of flesh and bone, because, he
said, what's more random than duplication? Reynaud didn't want
anything like that, and to avoid it, he conceived of a remarkable
device. Pay attention."

I had gone to Mireaux's with one single question in mind,
and had asked him that question upon arrival, and his lengthy
circumlocution was beginning to get under my skin. The old man,
absorbed in his own explanation, crossed his office again, with a
new reel in his hand. He placed it in the machinery. The image of
the portly man with the bowler hat disappeared and in his place
was another figure, uncomfortably similar, with a glistening face,
a troubled look, and a grayish tear rolling down his cheek.

"This is Émile Reynaud, the inventor," said Mireaux. "It's a self-portrait in motion. If you look closely, he has assumed the position of Galipaux with meticulous care, and is going to copy his gestures, but not his expressions. The image of Reynaud, in effect, is just like the other image: facing an imaginary sky, he raised his exhausted fingers and his lips defined themselves in pitiful or nostalgic ecstasy. It was the beginning of a speech. Galipaux," Mireaux continued, "had engendered that minstrel version of Umberto I, a malevolent rogue, without any other emotions than fury and violence, and Reynaud envisioned this other one, this version of a desperate and saddened loner. The replication of the movements is millimetrical, the discrepancy of the expressions diametrical. Now, look at what happens if we superimpose the images of the two reels. I'm going to leave this one here and put the other one back on. If we run the drums and cranks and align them just so, the figures will be projected at the same time. There it goes. Do you see how the graininess is different? Once superimposed, each one fills in the blanks of the other, and the figure becomes clearer. Yet, at the same time, the minuscule differences in proportion give the new face a ghostly air. Do you see?"

While Mireaux was speaking, a third face had begun to emerge on the screen, the product of the superimposition of the other two. It was spectral and implausible, the features diluted on the edges, as if submerged in a washbowl, but it was also unsettling. His torsion seemed to be the result of an inner struggle, the fierceness of his gestures born of doubt, and the arabesque shadow puppets on his hands could not hide their painful core of fear and temerity as they started to flail around his face. The implacable king was a coward, the autocrat a misanthropic child. Each of those gestures was a contradiction.

"Reynaud," the old man said, "never saw any success with this variation on his praxinoscope. It would require a Freud, perhaps, to get the public to see that these little self-contradicting figures, which seemed to act in spite of their feelings, through whose visible faces other complex multiform faces would emerge, were really more trustworthy, more akin to humanity."

"Interesting," I said, "but can we return to my question?"

Mireaux stopped the rotation of the cranks, and the enthusiastic-sorrowful face of Reynaud-Galipaux froze on the wall behind him. The moth fluttered in curlicues around the beam of light.

"I have already replied," said the old man. "I told you the other day that Juliana was, essentially, two women, and what I was referring to ought now to be quite clear. But you're not the type of person to get trapped by metaphors. That's your major difference from Daniel."

"But still," I contested, "this is not a metaphor. What you mean to say is that behind the Juliana I knew there hid another Juliana that I didn't know, that I only saw on the outside, let's say, on the surface."

"Well," said Mireaux, "that's obvious with regard to all the people you have met in your life, yourself included. The thing is, in this case, the notion that everyone has two faces is indeed a metaphor for something else, Gustavo. What I am about to tell you, on the other hand, is not," he said. "There were two Julianas in Daniel's life, and the other one is the key to everything that you want to uncover. The two of them lived in the same house. One Juliana died fourteen days before the other, which is the woman about whom you've inquired, Daniel's fiancée. The death of the one caused the death of the other. He was in love with both of them at once, yet loved neither of them separately. For Daniel, they were the two faces of one woman. The woman he longed to possess did not exist in his world. He longed to live, if you want to see it this way, with the stereoscopic image of Reynaud and Galipaux, not with either one of their poor, monochrome faces."

My ire waxed perplexity and then greater ire. I thought that only an indolent, bitter old man like Mireaux would think to pose riddles about something as important as this, and I was on the verge of telling him so when he let out a fragile cackle that hollowed into a paradiddle of hiccups and coughs, at which point he started up again the Optical Theater of the Luminous Shadows. In the glow of the light beam that shined in my eyes, I discerned the face of Mireaux.

Trapped in the clattering of the machine, his voice said, "This is no guessing game, Gustavo. You know the other woman. She never responded when you would call her Adela because that was not her name. Do you remember? Juliana's maid? Her namesake, the flirtatious and fussy girl who played deaf when you called her by the nickname her employer had forced on her. The second Juliana, the lover that Daniel himself had taken to live in the house of the first one, perhaps with the illusion that, when seen in the light of day, when placed in the right position, they might together embody the figure of the woman of his dreams."

At that moment, upon the profile on the screen and the feeble image of Mireaux, I intuited the levitating three-dimensional portrait of that other Juliana—Adela, the uncontrollable, smiley girl who seemed to be the only living animal in that house where Daniel and his fiancée walked in circles like lost souls doing their penance. I recalled Daniel's muted gestures, his incomprehensible anxiety each time the two women were together in the same place. And on top of that imaginary profile, I saw Daniel opening his fist to show Pastor the invisible knife he had used to kill her.

"Daniel," said Mireaux, "met the two of them during the same time period. Our friend was working here and the other one was only three or four blocks away, in a dim side street that you yourself showed Daniel for the first time, many years ago. She was a dancer, so to speak, in a real hole in the wall, and he wanted to get her out of there, but his curiosity got the better of him and, rather than rescuing her, he put her in the other one's house. Then he turned that house into the test tube that, as you know, met a fatal end. I cannot betray Daniel by telling you the rest of the story, Gustavo. But no matter how horrifying it may be for you to discover, as it was for me, that our friend is not a temperamental killer who struck only once in a fit of jealousy, but rather a killer who has killed at least twice, all the same you have to do it. I've already learned to live with that idea, and now it's your turn to unearth everything and understand it. Only one person will have no qualms about telling you the whole truth, as far as I know. Go down to the Biblio Path and ask Yanaúma."

SIXTEEN

"If you look at it today, you'd think it's an enormous coffin flipped over on its side, with the top swung open as a result of the fall. It's got an angular shape that makes it higher on the left side, over here, and an asymmetric gable roof, shorter toward the front wing and elongated toward the back, over here. Inside, you'll see it's divided in half by a stone wall now sealed in concrete, with covered spy-holes that were once used by guards during the early years. When they constructed this building, it wasn't a hospital. Almost three hundred years ago it was a mansion that, seen from the outside, used to look like a single impressive straw cube, stuccoed with quincha composite, decorated with friezes and engraved yellow flowers. On the inside, it was broken up into a myriad of small, identical rooms. The man who built it was a filthy-rich misanthrope, suspicious of everyone and everything, and he'd tremble when Indians, blacks, and mulattoes would congregate on the street, each time more intensely, each time more insolently, and so he decided to live separated from the city—because back then, this place was outside the city proper—and ordered his house be built next to the valley, upon a stony esplanade where, as he had confirmed, he would be able to obtain water by digging a couple of pumping wells.

"The man used to sleep alone in the house, every night in a different room, and during the day he'd allow only his servants to enter. Reposed and serene in the security of distance, he basked in his bitter loneliness for years on end; he'd send servants to the city to purchase provisions, and they'd return with urban and genteel news regarding new mayors, new streets, new viceroys, and recently published books, which the misanthrope refused to read. In fact, he never allowed a book to cross the threshold of his residence. But, after a while, the most fearful news imposed itself directly upon his senses.

"One autumn, on the balcony of one of his many bedrooms, he was able to confirm that the corrupt atmosphere of the city, with its recycled air, was not far off, that the babbling swarm of its citizens was wheezing ever closer. After only a few years, on the edges of the highest hill in the valley, the black profile of the city fatally began to emerge before his eyes, overrunning his old property line and headed for the countryside. Fortunately for him, the city wasn't expanding in a uniform circle, like the wave of an explosion, but rather pushing forward consistently and stretching into the great spiral avenue that stemmed from its center, popping up one-horse towns and opening alleyways in the intersections, teeming until it poured over the sides.

"Look, if this is the old man's house (this one here, you see?) and this was the valley (over here in the center), you can imagine that the city was in this area, farther away, and in the space between one and the other the spiral avenue continued to run, and each of its coils would curl closer to the man's estate. Do you see? The people built shacks and lined them up on horse paths that would later form entire neighborhoods of ruinous little cabins on the margins of that bustling road, in such a way that the boom became cyclical—with the houses came the noise, the commotion, the retinue of miserable city dwellers. But each time they seemed to have taken the final step in invading the misanthrope's stony esplanade and his private valley within the open valley, the avenue would continue its curve and wind around the other side of the hills, to form a new ring, growing closer, more distressing for him, but nonetheless tolerable.

"After several years, the slow procession returned and formed another ring, and then another, and one day the misanthrope, foreseeing that the next boom of strangers would reach his property and trap his mansion in unpleasant urban racket, concocted a plan to transform the house into a fort, raising walls around the rectangular plot of land that made up his premises. For months, he oversaw the progress of the construction. He stuck his head out of the windows of his twenty bedrooms to correct errors, pointed out dimensions and materials from a distance, gesturing with his ebony cane from some high gable, or exhaling commands and specifications through the peephole of a door on the ground floor, without ever stepping foot outside his refuge. When the construction was finished, the first droves of filthy gray people stained with blood and mud lined up along the front wall of the fort, alongside mules hauling carts filled with cane and mortar to erect new houses, and battalions of people dying from hunger in search of unclaimed lands between the city and the sea. The avenue had grown until it was finally stopped at the side wall of the gigantic house. Now that it had reached this obstacle in its path, and with the ever-so-long thicket behind the mansion, the avenue was forced to take a detour, which is why a second spiral emerged that curls in the opposite direction and, instead of opening up, closes in on itself, like the coiling of a serpent. It bestows on the modern city the shape of a circuit made of two spirals that just barely touch at that point. Come here, stand right here, look at it from above. Do you get it? It's in the shape of a figure eight: two centers, two spirals, one sole point in common, and on that point was the house where today you'll find the hospital.

"When the years of solitude turned into decades, the now feeble man waxed all the more extravagant. It was then that he ordered the land between the walls to be covered with roofs, concealing the courtyards and the esplanade. On the two sides of the original cube, he designed rows of similar rooms, following the path of two curving hallways, one on each side of the old house, under the giant roof, two oval passageways, two rings cinching ever tighter, two spirals that would each lead to a central courtyard, the only unroofed spaces in the entire complex, until his foreboding building began to portend the shape of the city nearly a century afterward. That's why the hospital is the way it is. Because it's a glimpse, a precognition, and at the same time, a puzzle. Do you see what I mean? It's hard without a map in front of your eyes. The city and the hospital are identical. You, because of your seclusion, have hardly lived in the city, but you're going to live in the hospital, which is why it's good for you to know this, to keep it in mind. Those who live in the city don't manage to understand it completely either; that's impossible.

"The city is divided in two, as is the hospital, and those who live on one side only in a blue moon manage to conceive an image of the other. Do you know why the hospital is divided like this? When the old man died, without children, without siblings, without anyone to carry on his name (he died one Saturday afternoon, and they found him Sunday morning, sitting on his bed, wearing nothing but boots which were apparently covered with mud from the thicket neighboring the fort), the mansion was taken over by the Church, and later by City Hall, which first turned it into a leper colony and then into a prison. During that time, on the streets of the city there had been battles, riots, and uprisings. The republic was founded and the wars multiplied. So, in one of their countless clashes, opposing forces were the inhabitants of both sides of the city, each army led by a strongman, each arguing for principles that were different in appearance, until the leaders made a pact and the conflict fizzled into a feeble, although for a time functional, coexistence. Peace, however, never did reach the prison.

"In there, the two armies continued their guerrilla warfare—stealthy attacks or unmasked skirmishes under the giant roof that covered the whole building—until one day the mayor decided to put an end to the fighting and, with this objective, ordered the construction of an impenetrable dividing wall. Then the entire place was split in two, traversed by that solid wall of granite and stone, and underneath a tunnel was dug that followed the same path in such a way that, whether aboveground or below, it was impossible to go from one side to the other except through the tiny door left for the guards to communicate. Ever since that moment, the prison—which had been the old man's house and, years later, the hospital—remained broken in two, and the inhabitants of both sides were forced to move about through only one passageway, each group trapped in its own spiral until the suffering came to an end, when absolution or death would claim them.

"So, over the course of half a century, this was a prison, and the great dividing wall separated the inhabitants of the west spiral from those of the east. Later on, for fifty years it was a hospital, with one ward for the contagious and another for low-risk patients. Those with scabies, the flu, warts, consumption, or syphilis would go to the first ward for a quick death or to infect the others. On the other side of the wall were pregnant women, patients with varicose veins, anemia, inflammations, et cetera. For the last five decades, it's been an asylum. The wall still divides the interned patients in half. And once you get there, you'll see just how. Actually, I could tell you quickly right now. When you're inside you may not perceive a difference. Did you notice what the asylum is called? It bears the name of the old man who built the house to begin with. At some moment, when it was changing from prison to hospital, a clerk, overwhelmed by all the registers, annals, and municipal documents, mistook the old anchorite for a philanthropist, and suggested they rename it, and ever since then the custom has stuck. Parks and boulevards bear that name and it often appears on the roster of the country's founders. But that's not important. Now, come over here. I need help picking this up. Take it by that edge and I'll grab this side. And off comes the roof. That's it. I think we can place it a little farther over there, next to your bed. There you go. Take off the sheets. Thanks. Whoops, not that far.

"So, without the roof, it's easier to appreciate the layout of the hallways, the rooms, and the two central courtyards. What I want you to understand, when you're living in the hospital, is that this wall that cuts everything in half isn't there by accident. It's there for a reason. Remember this: you must never try to get to the other side. It's dangerous. You're going to remember, right? You have to remember.

"Were you wondering why I went to the hassle of building this? Why with more details than ever, with greater precision, without forgetting a service door, the long encased windows, a tiny closet, the spring-loaded mousetrap? I'll tell you why. Because after all the wars, as you well know, there was an even longer war. Like those that came before it, it was fought in the city and its echoes bounced off the walls of this building. When the war came to an end, an ankylotic peace befell it—a fossilized peace made of lies—and this was where, by government decree, members of rival gangs were sent, leading the hospital to assign each gang to a ward. Those who didn't belong to either faction ended up going to one of them at random, and in this way they were victimized yet again. That population, in its entirety, predator and prey alike, has diminished over time, though. It's faded out, and the hospital has opened its doors to patients of any background by modifying its classification criteria. Now, in one wing there are the violent patients and in the other the nonviolent, so it no longer matters if there are events in their personal backgrounds that link them to the war. Two combatants from opposing armies may find themselves in the same ward, and sometimes they realize it; they perceive and intuit the differences, or a gust of incomprehensible hatred blows through them from some remote corner of their lives, or a distant voice simply tells them they must destroy the other, and, without understanding what this means, they do just that. As is to be expected, in the ward of violent patients the rules are very strict, so much so that those rumpuses are scarce, but they persist. What's more, two old enemies don't need to bump into each other for something terrible to happen. Everyone in that place is a potential killer.

"It pains me to say it, but, given the things you've done, you must go to that ward. That's why it's important for you to memorize everything I'm showing you. For that reason, and since I know these things amuse you, that they relax you, I've built this mock-up of the hospital. Look at it closely, I made it for you. I'm going to leave it here for you to study. Learn it by heart. Remember where you shouldn't stick your nose, the places you shouldn't go, the rooms you can hide away in and lock the bolts, and remember to turn all the keys the day you hear something strange, or if someone looks at you cross, or if someone wants to start something with you. And above all, remember what I told you. Never try to get to the other side. If it's not dangerous for you, it'll be dangerous for everyone else.

The nights find the Antiquarian the same as the mornings: folios on the floor, xylographs and illuminated manuscripts in the study, maps of the sky and the earth and blueprints of buildings that consist of a basement and an attic without anything in between. The Antiquarian beholds the designs, the scraps of tissue paper pinned to a wall with four thumbtacks in each corner, the miniature figurines of whales, tritons, and amphisbaenas—some of them sitting in my audience this afternoon—that adorn the legends at an acute angle on each map. Icons of precaution and warning. Gripping the magnifying glass, his trembling fingers announce the moment of departure out onto the spiral street for a walk to the house or motel. There, the question again is heard. My name is Juliana, what's yours? And tonight, finally, the moment is right, and he responds. My name is Daniel—I'm the Antiquarian—and he walks behind her to the room made of fog and reflections, and he observes Juliana's skin, which, tanned and dried and sliced with finesse, would make fine paper, and for the first time—the sound of a drop of water oozing into another, the glow of a candle that's never been lit—he discovers that there are things in the world that aren't in the books.

SEVENTEEN

"But, according to the sign, Tres Espadas is a one-way street."

"That depends."

"Depends on what?"

"On which way you're facing when you pass the sign."

Twenty years after my first visit, the street parallel to the spiral avenue was more babelic, more far-fetched, still held captive by the same book dealers, or by their children or grandchildren. The sidewalk was almost invisible beneath a layer of dust, oil, and remnants of food; the sky above it, lower and more oppressive than usual. The clouds, viscous as petroleum, seemed nearly solid and appeared to be filled with the dead bodies of birds by the hundreds that had died mid-flight and were about to fall onto the road the next time it rained—an enormous amulet of white feathers and bones, hanging precariously over the city. On the way from my house to that neighborhood, the streets were changing, renouncing normality and transforming into a pulpy quarter of hovels that were previously in shambles and now resembled nightmares, torture, vengeance, prison. Droopy-eyed people stood gaping from the doorways of buildings, hardly breathing, their gazes averting mine each time I looked at them, not threateningly or frightfully but suspiciously, as though they thought it was my intention to steal the password to their existence. The street vendors on the divider, in turn, looked friendly and aggressive at the same time.

Yanaúma was also someone else. Two decades later, this farcical, large-framed man had become a mummy of himself; the patch of black hair was a bunch of split threads, and in the place where he used to keep the skull, on the table in front of his stand, there was a bust of Goethe, sculpted from a coconut shell. I had seen the guy many times over recent years, but never had I perceived his deterioration. The only thing that was the same on that street were the pyramids, the stockpiles, the mountains, the columns of books that rose up from everywhere and seemed to bulge in front of the pedestrians. Yanaúma's voice sounded like an English horn, and his black-fingernailed hands accompanied the rhythm of his words.

"Daniel," Yanaúma said, "used to come by here three, four, five times a week. For years he would scour the shelves and the mounds of books, paying uncanny attention to detail, as if he were trying to take a census of every single volume. And I would watch him ferreting here and there, and I focused on his beady eyes, on how they would suddenly turn away from the bookcases, and his pupils would grow larger in the presence of some stranger who passed by him, and how he would suddenly let them fall upon someone, as if he were waiting to receive a greeting or be let in on an inside joke, an amicable chitchat, or the kind of gossip that abounds in places like this.

"So it was that we became friends," said Yanaúma, "because, like you, Gustavo, I too gained access to his loneliness and granted him access into mine; and because we quickly realized that we were suffering the same compulsion for history, we would pass the time telling each other stories that we fabricated on the fly, both of us knowing that the value did not reside in their references or accuracy, but in their parabolic capacity, in the number of knots there were to untie from each story in order to turn it into a continual and linear sequence, with a comprehensible message. Between us only silence was forbidden," said Yanaúma. "It must have been some kind of sickness, huh?"

"Yeah," I replied, after wondering for a few seconds if it was really a question. "I mean, no. Rather, there are lots of people who speak compulsively, but very few of them are pathological." I started to feel how ridiculous my answer was, but I didn't stop. "It tends to be a feature of hypomania, and what's odd about it is that hypomania is a symptom of depression, but almost impossible to distinguish from pure happiness."

"So then what we had must have been hypomania," Yanaúma said, "because, while Daniel and I were talking, I never knew if we were sad or happy."

"You know what I want to talk about, right?" I asked him.

"I think I do, yes, but I'd rather you tell me clearly," Yanaúma replied.

I summarized my conversation with Mireaux for him. He stayed quiet for a few seconds, rhythmically tapping his right thumb with his four other fingers.

"Did he tell you that it was a shock for him to find out that Daniel had killed two people?" Yanaúma smiled. "Mireaux is not the kind of guy to be shocked by this, I should say."

"What do you mean?" I asked.

"Nothing," said Yanaúma, and he raised his thick eyebrows and widely opened up his eyes, only to add that the rest was true. "Daniel killed two women, and I knew this as soon as it happened, but his partners knew this too, and they kept their mouths shut as tight as I've kept mine. Now they have been slowly nudging you toward me, so that I take on the task of revealing the dark side of this affair. That's these guys for you. They always have friends who, beneath the surface, are servants who make sure the dirty laundry gets washed. There you have it. You know about one part of the story: Daniel met Juliana at *La Verdad*, and they soon got engaged, which excited him during the early years but confused him over time, when he discovered that pleasing Juliana entailed abandoning his isolation, socializing with more friends than he had ever had in his life, striking up trivial conversations with people who were totally different from him, confronting his father, who didn't think Juliana was up to par with his rich, intelligent son, and doing so without overexciting his mother, thrilled at the prospect of a wedding for her boy hermit, who'd never had a single girlfriend."

I impatiently interrupted Yanaúma to tell him that I indeed knew all that.

"And now you also know, from Mireaux," he said, "that Daniel tried to keep up appearances in his relationship, but little by little he gave in to the absurd temptation, or am I wrong? And you also know why this was a temptation. Let me tell you how it began. Pastor, his partner, set out to make Daniel believe his situation was normal—the monotony of any couple—that things were always like that, and all he needed was to have some fun, not leave Juliana, but complete what he was getting from that bond by adding a parallel life to it, one with greater risks, more freedom, less oppression. And Daniel, numb to his feelings, believed him, maybe without knowing it, or perhaps he wanted to believe, and he went in search of that thing, precisely what he was missing, without knowing what it was. Pastor made it his personal mission to take Daniel to singles bars, pubs, and nightclubs. And when they would go to one of these, no matter how disgusting it was—oh, the things Pastor would tell me!—Daniel further embellished that attitude of intellectual severity that grips him whenever he's nervous. You know what I'm talking about. He would go to places that stank of cheap perfume, liquor, and disinfectant, radiating the same seriousness as he did when he entered the university library, and he'd look at the women in the bar, at the women who were dancing on the dance floor, or leaning against a column, at the women who pulled their heads into their shells off in some corner, with their legs enmeshed in everyone else's, who looked at themselves in the mirror, and at the pairs of women who had their arms around each other and would laugh with tremendous cackles, or into the other's ear, as if all those bodies before him were documents, and he would sit on a pleather sofa, with a drowsy gaze from the red lamps and vaporous shades, to wait for one of them to approach him. Then he would try to strike up an impractical conversation, in a language that sounded ridiculous to them, and when he decided to touch them, he placed a finger on the girl's throat and quickly slid it down, as if he were cutting her in two, or as if, with that outstretched finger, he were skimming through the index of an encyclopedia. Later, when the drinks had gone to his head, Daniel would revert to his old routine of telling stories. And, as he slipped along the gravelly slope into the depths of one of them, then fell into a trance, the women would look at him like the wacko everyone took him for and they'd leave him there talking to himself, translating into words his awkward excitement, the squeamishness of that desire he'd never been able to assimilate, as he defended himself against normality from behind that wall of tales.

"Pastor insisted, nonetheless," said Yanaúma, "until he turned Daniel into a regular at several of those mildewy, pestilent little palaces, and Pastor would place on his lap one girl after the next, an assembly of robotic and boisterous females, orphaned adolescents, penniless students, country girls lost in urbanity, single mothers who would doze off and wake up startled a thousand times throughout the course of the evening only to then cook and bathe the kids before waiting in line at the bank and the store, and by night slip on their hand-sewn vampiress outfits in order to go to the nebulous carnival of some nightclub, and there find, slouched over on a bench in the corner, that lonely little man who would suddenly start babbling some inexplicable speech, while he watched them join him, with their fascinated faces, motioning with their fingers to each other that this guy was certifiably crazy, and that someone should take their spot. Another one would always show up, sit next to him, rub his neck with her hand, run a couple of chewed fingernails through his hair, along his nape, and all this repeated, identically, pathetically, until one evening a girl came up to him and did not follow the ritual. Daniel was surprised when she told him to keep talking—'I like to listen'—to let her nuzzle up to him for a bit—'I've been on my feet all night, I haven't slept in two days, so tell me another story'—the rough, thick mascara and the violet lipstick, dried and streaked on her lips, her eyes a greenish brown under her thick eyebrows, her fingernails peeled back and tinged with blood, a turquoise miniskirt and shoes, and a transparent black blouse, dotted with sequins that stuck to the sofa each time she moved. 'Tell me you have another story'—she had never spoken like this before—'and I can tell you mine too, it's been a long time since I've had someone to tell them to, if you want we can get out of here, somewhere else would be more comfortable, it doesn't matter if you only want to talk.' It had been a long time since he had conversed with anyone.

"That girl was the other Juliana. Daniel didn't know her name for a while—no one at those places uses a real name, to confess it means removing the mask, to stop being womanizers and seducers and become lonely men and prostitutes. So he began learning about her life little by little, first by patronizing that place, and then by calling her on the phone to see if she would meet him in a motel, in the evening, in one of those small old squares with tall, skinny houses with tiles calcined by years in the white-hot sun and saline air, amid the heady vapor of half-bankrupt restaurants on every corner of the city's streets, and that fog of broken crystals that rolls in each evening from the beaches below to the streets downtown. 'Now it's my turn. Let me tell you my story'—that's what the other Juliana must have said to him during one of those evenings," said Yanaúma, and he kept staring at the bust of Goethe upon the plywood table, flaring his nostrils as if he were sniffing the scent of an animal among the people in front of his stand, and then he said, "I don't know what kind of resemblance the words I'm about to tell you will have in comparison to those that she said to Daniel, and Daniel to Pastor, and Pastor to me." Yanaúma lowered his eyes and started to nibble on a piece of torn skin at the cuticle of his little finger, and he began to speak in the voice of a drunkard, saliva accumulating between his tongue and palate, sticking half a finger in his mouth, biting and biting. "'Now it's my turn, let me tell you my story,' said the girl one of those evenings.

"She and Daniel had found a colorless motel on the east corner of the small square, behind the library, two dozen bland yet clean rooms: a double bed, a stand with the Bible and a telephone book, and the remote control to a television that was no longer there. Daniel kissed her between the legs, and then moistened her nipples with the tip of his tongue, repeating on the body of his lover the lessons learned on the body of his fiancée. And even though, with that first Juliana, his fiancée, on the enormous bed in that house he had rented for her, he would feel the thunderous pulse of blood filling his veins and would want to prolong the sex for pleasure, but also in order not to reach the emptiness that overcame him at the end, on that stiff bed in the motel, upon that tumorous little mattress with this new Juliana, Daniel was feeling desire but also haste, the urge to be there forever and at once the need to finish quickly in order to wrap her in his arms, untie her braids of black hair from behind her ears, and tell her something only to later find himself listening to what she had to say. 'Let me tell you my story,' the girl was saying." That's how she said it that time, according to Yanaúma.

"In one of the identical rooms of that motel, she was naked on her back, her torso propped up by her elbows, her hands playing with the skin on her neck, Daniel, curled around a pair of pillows, attentive, waiting. She said to him, 'I'm from a very small town, quite far from here,' where her parents had been farmers, not the poorest of the poor, but very poor nonetheless, and Daniel kissed her dried hands with hardened hangnails and shiny skin. She continued to speak. 'My mom was over forty years old when I was born,' and she said that her father was even older, but very strong, and that aside from the land he farmed, he had a thousand different jobs. 'He'd buy rice and milk in a neighboring town and would return through the boroughs to sell his goods, on trips that would last two days, with bags and sacks of rice and milk on the back of a burro, one of my brothers as a helper, and he'd bring achira roots for Grandma, my mom's mother, the oldest person in that town where people died before growing old,' she said. And Daniel put his thighs over hers, lying there face-to-face, that wide face of hers, with eyes that would change color in the light, and he continued listening. 'There were six kids in my family, but two died of typhus. We'd spent two whole days searching for lice all over the house and in the hides of our animals to avoid contagion, but nothing—two died,' she said. 'That time my mother almost died too. Given the future that awaited her, dying right then wouldn't have been a bad option,' and Daniel closed his eyes and slid four fingers between her left arm and her side, and confirmed that his fingers fit perfectly between the grooves formed in her skin by the protuberance of her ribs, and he left his hand there, clenched and still, in order to make certain that she still existed, that what was speaking was not a bodiless voice. He listened, feeling the rest of the story invade him through his ears and nose, warming his body, and he kept quiet, paying attention. 'That's why there were only four of us when the war began,' her voice said, 'the only boy was fourteen and, of the three girls, I was the youngest, eight years old, and Mom and Dad and Grandma were still around when the soldiers took over the town, though it seems like a lie now.

"'It was the town from the stories people were talking about in those days, and even months earlier. From neighboring hamlets people would come with tales of spirits and headless bodies, of ghosts that would become corpulent in the cold of evening and multiplied among the sown fields and puddles in the pasturelands, and would suddenly form an enormous circle, surrounding the houses, singing in unison monotonous songs with one single repeated phrase. They'd never leave without first slitting numerous throats. They chopped them up with hatchets or machetes, cutting off their arms or slicing their mouths through their cheeks, so that the dead, afterward, seemed to be laughing with those piñata expressions lingering on their faces. We hadn't seen the ghosts, but only heard the stories from those who came to escape from them when they passed through town, scattering in all directions. They were almost always children with horrified faces or old women with bloody scabs on their shins and gashes, scratches, and burns on their hands and feet. For a long time the war was just this for us: rumors, tales of men transformed into beasts, stories that old ladies and orphans would repeat, news of towns destroyed and mass graves filled, with priests shot mid-mass and women locked up in barracks and raped by entire platoons—stories I'll tell you

later, if you'd like to hear them,' the girl said. And Daniel passed
his hand over her forehead and said that, yes, he did, and she went
on to tell."

"'We used to hear them as if they were pieces of a distant
world,' she said, 'as if something had exploded nearby and the
ashes were raining onto our town, carried by the wind. But all
this suddenly changed,' she said. 'One evening a boy arrived on
the main road, dragging his dog by the ear. The dog was a rag of
coagulated blood, with a large, round orifice in the middle of its
belly. It was nothing but fur and hide and a shell of rib bones and
limbs that hung limp. Though its head was still intact, the rest of
him didn't look like a dog, but rather the costume of a dog. Some
loose entrails, however, were still bouncing around inside his body.
They'd carved him like a pumpkin, and what he was carrying in
his stomach, according to those who approached him, were two
human hearts. The boy was dragging the dog by the ear, down the
road, and that's how he reached the center of town, right in front of
our house—a white scab under his nose, his hair the color of dirt,
his lips cracked from a bloody lashing. He was mumbling something
but no one understood him. My mother and father made him let go
of the body, took him into the house, and with a wet cloth washed
his face and eyes, which were covered by a crust thick like tears
of mud. The dog was left on the ground outside,' said the girl,"
according to Yanaúma, who was toying with the bust of Goethe and
raising his eyes every so often to confirm that I was still there. His
voice gurgled untiringly, watery, like the black current of a creek.

"The animal bore the appearance of a rag, according to the girl,
and Daniel was listening but his attention oscillated between the
story and the prostrated girl's dark folds of skin. 'The dog looked
like a doll tossed next to the poker into the pile of charred logs
near the stove where Grandma used to bake her achira cookies

for Sunday, when she would try to sell them to people on their way back from mass in a nearby town. After a while, the boy went outside and, walking slowly, picked the dog up again by his ear and repeated the same entangled phrase that no one managed to understand. He stayed there for several hours. My father returned from the fields and, when they told him, he went to the boy and again made him let go of the animal. The boy obeyed without putting up a fight. My father carried the dog and placed it on top of the stove, and with two fingers opened the hole in the stomach to confirm what they had told him—there were two human hearts. He looked at everyone else with an expression of "Now what are we going to do with this?" What do you do with something like that? A few minutes later the soldiers arrived.

" 'They descended down the same road as the boy. There were twelve of them in all. The afternoon wasn't cold, but the collars of their jackets were pulled up to their noses and they were wearing balaclavas to cover their faces. For that reason, from a distance they looked like twelve crosses nailed into the hillside. They continued to slowly come down the gutted slope, spangled with thistle, burrs, and stands of dead tree trunks burned dry by the most recent drought. They approached in silence, and when they were close we saw that they had two limp bodies on the back of a burro, bodies whose arms dangled toward the ground as if wanting to grab between their fingers the wildflowers growing on the shoulder of the road. When they arrived at the flats where the town starts, one of the men split off from the others and walked toward us, his rifle nestled on his forearm, with the sight facing down, a long butcher's knife in the other hand. He walked to my father and with a surly voice asked, *What's that you've got there?* pointing with his eyes to the dog on top of the stove. *Nothing,* said my father, *a dead dog a boy brought from God knows where.* The man grabbed the dog and stuck his hand into the hole in the dog's belly and bent over to vomit. The sheep got spooked and trotted off toward the row of houses. The man walked back to the burro and untied the ropes around the two bodies; each of them fell on a different side of the animal, getting soaked on the edge of a ditch near where my grandmother, mother, siblings, and a group of neighbors were standing. Then he grabbed one of the bodies by the feet and dragged it until it was next to the other one, with the help of two soldiers who were moving like ghosts, without a sound, with an expression of shock and desolation stuck on their faces. The cadavers remained belly up, their chests coated in black and brown mud, two filthy, grimy pigs resembling half-made clay figurines. At the level of the heart they had two deep holes, like cracked-open skulls. Two sandy, fractured skeletons, wrapped in skin that looked yellow where their military uniforms ended, whose misery the man seemed to emphasize with his outstretched hand: *And you're gonna tell me that this isn't anything either?* he asked, without looking at my father but addressing him with a raspy, crackling scream. Seemingly possessed, he skipped to the stove and took the dog as if he were carrying his dead child, with a broth of tears pouring down his cheeks. He walked with it to where the cadavers were lying and thrust his hand in between the rib cage of the animal and one by one removed the hearts, which looked like two filthy stumps and blades of grass, and put them back inside the bodies, panting with nausea. The soldiers turned away so they didn't have to see.

"'That afternoon,' said the girl," Yanaúma continued, "'the officer killed my father with a single slice to the throat, and the soldiers did the same thing to the rest of the men of the town, including the youngest boys, among them my brother and the boy with the dog. They let the women weep in mourning for a while and then forced them to dig a deep ditch about a quarter mile from town. They threw the dead in there and then shot the widows, the daughters, the granddaughters, and tossed in the rest of the bodies too. My mother was the last one to go; they had to pull me from her arms. I saw her thrown into the ditch with a hole in her forehead. They let me and another girl live, I don't know why. They wanted to rape us, but we were too little and it was hard for them to get inside our bodies, which turned iridescent with bruises, scrapes, bites, knife-cuts, and the marks of sharp fingernails and hungry claws. When they left, hours later, pulling along a line of goats and carrying six hens under their arms, they didn't discuss whether to take us with them or kill us as well, they simply left. *And what are you crying for, huh?* one of the soldiers said to me. And they left us in that cadaverous hamlet with two pigs and a wounded rooster. That was the first day of my history.

" 'The other girl and I,' she said," according to Yanaúma, " 'spent the night in my house, stunned and silent, without looking at each other, and without even talking. The next morning we knew that we'd have to gather the animals and walk in the direction of the town behind the hills. There was an icy sun that day. The flowers on the road looked like green and yellow crystals, and the wind brushed against the grass on the mountainsides. That's what I remember most: we didn't know how to explain to the neighboring town everything that had happened to us. From then on, it's hard to tell how long we spent at each place, or through which towns we passed. No one wanted to take responsibility for us beyond giving us shelter for a couple of days, some meager plates of leftover food, permission to sleep in barns next to henhouses or in dilapidated sheds that seemed like they'd crumble if the wind blew too hard. In a larger town, the other girl managed to get room and board in a house in exchange for washing the laundry, sweeping the stubborn dust that fell upon the floors and stuck to the walls, and preparing what few meals she knew how to fry or bake or boil. But I, on the other hand,' said the girl to Daniel, while he was caressing her blackish tufts of hair, 'I remained adrift, searching for a job in the shanties of a miserable neighborhood, wandering through filthy streets and lightless plazas, where night fell in the middle of the afternoon, when a breeze of human dust and ground-up stones picked up and blew against the weeds of the alleys and intensified the stench of dog piss and burro hair that was already infesting the air. I don't know how long, maybe years, I spent living off the irritated charity of shopkeepers and the grumpy condolences of pedestrians, chewing half-eaten bread and leftover vegetables that I used to find on abandoned unfinished plates in the only place to eat, at the town's only inn, until one day an Army truck passed through picking up unaccompanied boys and girls who were wandering aimlessly, and they made me get in and took me to a shelter for orphans of the war. I stayed there for three years and three months, counted to the day, living with those other miniature monsters that some soldiers had left in the hands of other soldiers, in a greasy citadel of dirty animals whose faces were covered with drool and streams of tears and snot, who would learn to read and write and recite the names of the heroes, the regions of the country, the symbols of the Nation, the long litany of military defeats and the nighttime prayers, during which we had to pray for the soldiers to win the war and for the others to be left without even a scrap of living skin on the face of the earth. One mud-colored afternoon when the truck that was unloading dry goods for the kitchen arrived, I escaped with the help of a little black-faced soldier who took mercy on my gesture of pain and asked me to go down on him, for a long time, before telling me that I could get in the back and that, if anyone discovered me, he'd have nothing to do with it. In the clattering truck, after two days and nights on the road, I reached the city. My first memory of it is the entrance of the giant spiral avenue that closes in on itself, like the coiling of a serpent, and the demonic roar of startled shrieks and booming voices of combat incarnate, the bestial vroom of the cars, the febrile expression on the faces of people in the street, and the immediate impression that this world was worse than the world of the war. That's just what this city is. And here I've stayed since, reduced to nothing, without an education, without anyone to hear my history, without relatives, without anything else but my name and my face and the functions of my body. I knew how to walk, to sleep and remember. I knew how to sweat, cry, and cough. I knew how to clean my fingernails, pray in two languages, and kill weasels by smashing them with a rock. I knew how to do what I had done to the soldier and I was able to learn other things that were done with the legs and the hands, and by the age of sixteen I was a dancer at a disgusting saloon in the red-light district, by the age of seventeen I had my own clients—a bunch of old men with acne-eaten faces and horny little boys who wanted their first time to be with a faceless woman, one without an address—and at the age of eighteen La Japonesita took me to her bar and turned me into what I am today, into what you have between your hands.'

"That's what the girl said," Yanaúma continued with a grimace, "and Daniel listened to her like you're listening to me, Gustavo, with his ears ashamed and his gaze divided between pity and contrition."

"And what happened next?" I asked.

"You already know what happened. Daniel fell in love with her and wanted to take her away from that labyrinth of moldy meats, thighs, and folded bills, but at the same time, perhaps when he discovered that her real name was Juliana, and seeing in her the portents of fate, he came up with the stupid, admirable idea of bringing her to live in the house with the other Juliana, his fiancée, who changed the girl's name to Adela and took her in as a maid without suspecting a thing, or blinding herself to it so that Daniel could carry out that loathsome experiment of having both of them under the same roof. After a year, as Mireaux told you, both of them were dead, the girl first and two weeks later the other one, the official Juliana."

"Why did he kill them?" I asked.

"I can only speculate," said Yanaúma. "Maybe the girl couldn't completely leave behind the customs of her prior life and provoked in Daniel a simple fit of jealousy. Perhaps, more obviously, she rebelled against that new servitude and wanted to get out of there. Perhaps Daniel wasn't able to support the imminence of their separation and preferred to abolish the mere possibility. Perhaps the other Juliana discovered something and that's also why he had to end it with the girl, or it could be that killing her was a natural step, that Daniel saw the two crimes as one single indivisible action, the course of things once the girl was dead. Beyond that, I don't know."

Upon the plywood tabouret Yanaúma placed the Goethe bust, which he had been playing with throughout the course of this account. In the neighboring kiosks, the merchants were beginning to gather their merchandise. The plastic tarps were being lowered, and they were carelessly storing the books in wooden boxes and inhospitable chests of corrugated cardboard, and exchanging words about plans for later that night and the following morning.

One of the merchants, the closest to me, was a husky kid whose skin was speckled with pinkish pocks. As he passed between us, with a pack of cloth-wrapped books on his shoulder, he said to Yanaúma, "See you tomorrow, Cabecita Negra," and to me he shot a glance that said goodbye, lowering and then reluctantly raising his eyebrows. A fine, anemic mist barraged the divider of the avenue and the row of restaurants on both sides let heady clouds slip by. The fleeting city of books was rapidly dismantling itself, and on its deserted shores remained the other city, no more concrete or less out of breath, with a patina of grease crawling down its walls like vines.

Yanaúma repeated, "Beyond that, I don't know," and, rising to his feet, he pulled open a little drawer from the stand under the tabouret where he kept his locks and chains, and he began to place his books in trunks and coffers with scrupulous care. I picked up on his signal and said goodbye without further questions. Crossing the street, I had to dodge the stunts of a group of clowns in raggedy costumes interrupting the flow of traffic with acrobatic leaps and contortions. When I was nearing the corner, a hand grabbed my elbow and slightly tugged, and when I turned around, in front of me there was a pockmarked face. It was the husky kid who had only minutes ago said goodbye to us.

"Cabecita Negra hasn't told you even half of what he knows."

I stalled in responding to him, due to my concern, but also due to the vague yet shrill din of the merchants and pedestrians crammed on the sidewalk.

"Cabecita Negra knows much more," the guy repeated, kicking aside a dog that had started to hump his leg. "But I too know part of the story. And if you're interested, I can tell you. Seven blocks from here, heading down this same cross-street, there's a bar called Mikrokosmos. Do you know it? Be there at ten tonight and I'll speak with you."

EIGHTEEN

Daniel had been right. The afternoon I returned to the hospital wanting to speak with him, the secretary at reception motioned for me to wait and disappeared through the hallway, only to return a moment later with a fainthearted smile, saying, "Today it will not be possible, sir—try again tomorrow," and when I demanded to talk to someone who could explain the reasons why, the woman did not lead me to a doctor, but rather asked a caretaker to escort me to a small and foul-smelling office, which was accessed by descending a stairway at the side of the cafeteria and continuing down a straight corridor, so long that it made me feel like I was escaping the hospital through a tunnel dug over the course of many years of clandestine work. As I entered that nebulous office with air smelling of insecticide, I saw, up above, three little windows crossed by bars and, through their glow, I noticed the feet and legs of pedestrians on the street. Darkened by the contrast of the daylight, the objects in the room became brown and vaporous. Little by little, I discerned various stacks of papers on the desk and then the silhouettes of two men on the opposite side of the room, standing in the corner. I realized that I was in the office Daniel had described, the place where they had interrogated him. My eyes instinctually scanned over the place in search of the skull, which, at least at first sight, was nowhere to be found.

"My name is Vicario," said one of the silhouettes. "Captain Vicario. I'm sorry to inform you that there is no chance for you to see your friend this afternoon."

"It's really not that important," I replied.

"Oh, it's not? So then?"

"No, I just want to make sure Daniel is okay, to see if he needs anything," I said.

"Besides a lawyer?" Vicario replied, as he raised a hand and began picking at his face. "Or, are you a lawyer?"

"I'm not," I said. He made an ambiguous face, as if he had detected a mite in his pores and was at once filled with pleasure and repulsion by the idea of extracting it.

The other man, behind him but nearby, looking away from us both, seemed to be picking his nose.

"So if you're not a lawyer, then what are you?"

"What am I?"

"Right, what are you?"

"I'm a linguist," I said.

"A linguist?"

"A psycholinguist."

"A *psycho*-linguist."

"Yes, language problems."

"Ah, language problems," he repeated, and he let out the warble of a humorless chuckle.

In the tremor of the other man's shoulders, still turned away from us, I noted that he was chuckling too, but silently.

"And do you resolve the problems?" Vicario asked.

"I study them," I said.

"But you don't resolve them?"

"Sometimes I do."

The footsteps of the people on the sidewalk tapped away like the fingernails of an impatient hand.

"And what language problem does your friend suffer from?" he asked.

"None—it's not that."

"But you want to know if he's okay, or if he needs anything, isn't that right?"

"That's right," I said.

"Why wouldn't he be okay?"

"No, it's not that," I replied. "It's not that important."

"I see. And is there anything else I can do for you?" Vicario asked, and he took a step forward into the cascade of perpendicular light falling through the upper window. The other man walked in the opposite direction, his profile blending into the shadows.

I said yes, I was interested in seeing three patients, and I removed from my pocket the list Daniel had given me, unfolding it to read aloud the names. The captain reached out his arm, taking another step forward to grab the paper, and only then, when he was so close, did I notice the blotches on the back of his hand and, between his fingers, the white spots of psoriasis, which were making his skin peel.

"And why do you want to talk to those kooks?" Vicario asked. He was a man of my stature, neither heavyset nor slim. (A fat cop and a skinny one, Daniel had said.) On top of his head, the clump of salt-and-pepper hair split into several greasy clots that framed his face and in between his eyes and on his temples he had two enormous pink blotches, like a cat with scabies. (The psoriatic cop, Daniel had called him.)

I explained my friend's request to him.

"Look," he said, "I don't think you're going to gain anything by speaking with these kooks, but you're not going to lose much either, except your time. Anyway, it could be entertaining, and, since my primary mission these days is to pass the time, I'll allow you to speak to them, but only in my presence."

And I said, pointing with my chin to the silhouette of the other man, "I have no problem with you and your partner supervising the interviews."

Vicario pulled a rusty chain hanging from the ceiling between the two of them, and the livid glow of fluorescent lights illuminated the room.

"I don't have a partner," said the captain, "and believe you me, with the names you have on that paper, I doubt that what you're going to get will be 'interviews.'"

And he turned on his heels toward the desk, while in the corner behind him I caught sight of a very long, narrow, vertical mirror stuck to the side of a filing cabinet.

Pretending to have no concerns, I looked a while longer in order to verify that we were alone, then sat down in the second chair, in front of him. The door through which I had entered was the only one in the office.

"Do you want me to start calling them or do you have preparations to make beforehand?" he asked.

"No, you can go ahead and call them whenever you want," I said.

"Anyway," he replied, "I'm going to have them bring their medical histories, in case they may be of some use to you." Vicario grabbed a pack of cigarettes from the filing cabinet. He placed a cigarette between his teeth and brought a lit match to his mouth, and then, in the orange sphere of the flame, I focused on his swollen lips, covered by glistening, colloidal spores, canker sores, and blisters like wounds of boiling water. (Two policemen dressed in street clothes, Daniel had said: the first one with ulcerous lips, the second with patches of psoriasis on the back of his hands and on his eyebrows. Vicario, obviously, was both.)

"One more thing," I said.

"What's that?"

"I need to record the interviews, if that's not a problem."

"Record them?"

"Yeah, I highly doubt that the conversations—if they are in fact conversations, as you yourself have said—will end up being immediately indicative of anything. It's more likely that I'll have to listen to them many times before getting something clear out of them."

That night, in effect, I had to do just that. I detest the static hours at home; I'd rather insomnia enter and exit my body without pushing me through the stage of pills, of tossing and turning in bed. I even have a list of places where I go to let time drain without welling up inside me. I stopped halfway down the road between the hospital and my apartment at one of them, a little café called the Halfmoon, a quiet place run by two sisters. They are quite young, and twins, but, due to the anorexia of one of the sisters, side by side they look like the same person before and after death. I ordered a coffee, and a skeletal hand placed it on my table. I put on my headphones to transcribe the first conversation.

The scene from that afternoon gradually started reconstructing itself, traveling from my ears to my memory. Vicario had occupied a bench on the side, next to the door of the office, and a nurse brought in, one after another, the three patients. The first I had seen before, a woman I met in the hallway when I had just entered the ward, the first day I visited. "Here even light lives on," she had said that time, and now her little androgynous head appeared in the office with the same greeting. "Here even light lives on," she said, glaring at the fluorescent light on the ceiling. She grabbed a chair from alongside the desk, as if to sit on it, though she did not, and then, still standing, she saw the recorder on the desk and reached her two hands toward the machine, suddenly opening and closing her fists, her fingers in a convex curve, stretched out with great effort, her hands like two starfish, and on her face the expression of a proud illusionist. Then she raised her eyes and did not take them off the fluorescent light until we finished speaking. She must have been younger than thirty, but her hair was gray, and in the bags under her eyes the wrinkles formed a fold of mole-splattered flesh. Her eyes, on the other hand, maintained an infantile glow. Her voice on the tape was a uniform, serial cluck, like the rumbling of a broken-down motor, made up of short phrases, without intonation. A list of words: *here, even, light, lives, on*.

"Do you know what I want to talk about?" I asked.

She consented with her eyes and nodded her head. "Yes, even still I know, now or what?" she said, and in a lower voice she added a phrase that seemed like an apology: "The hours end fatally, inadvertently, and nobody cares enough, exactly over fire dangles another name, in eternal limbo." Then she fell silent, retracting her parted lips to reveal the root of her fangs.

Vicario scratched his cheek, and he laughed, an arbitrary cackle without a cause, almost a hiccup, which on the tape blended in with the barking of a stray dog, and he muttered, "Do you really think this is useful?"

I concentrated on the woman again.

"Think about the day when they found the girl dead," I said, "Do you remember that day? Do you remember her that day?"

Vicario rested his head in both his hands.

The woman nodded again, "This here is silence, is sadness," she said. "This, his earnest knife edge you think hasn't a tang. Yes, our understanding aims recklessly, even looking on or knowing inside . . ."

Before she could finish her phrase, I asked her to tell me something more specific, something from that day in particular. The woman did not like that I interrupted her—she closed her eyelids and her mouth contorted in a furious expression. "Nothing goes forth openly, right?" she asked, showing me the empty palm of her hand. I asked her to calm down and repeated the question. She paid me no attention. "Now," she said, "our window, a certainty. Hollow, anomalous, naked griffons, eternal pilgrims loom under some oblivion, never entering."

I repeated my question and once again she paid it no attention, and from that point forward, the tape contained only a brief monologue that the woman cyclically recited, starting over from the beginning each time she reached the end. "Just go!" she began. "Zechariah portends verdicts, maybe, possibly, perhaps, lunatic!" She pronounced the words carefully, opening up gaps between them. "God plays, smiling usward. Xenophobes play, queerly. Beasts!" Her hands possessed a rhythm that was absent in her voice. "Mimic the zephyr! Placidly vaporize good Jehovah! Originate entirely cloistered from us sinners."

Vicario yawned and continued to scratch his cheek.

"Benevolent Zechariah," the woman said, stretching out a finger to point at the captain, but without turning her eyes away from the light, "blessed my uterus in felicity, sorority, fraternity . . ." And then, with an exaltation that modified the volume but not the bone-dry tone of her voice on the tape, she uttered, "Jehovah told peasants, old farmers, jailed outside, crucify! Flesh under Xanthippe's fire fears others."

Vicario banged the table with his hand and walked to the door. He called the nurse to ask her to take the woman away and bring in the next patient, and he looked at me without saying anything, a sardonic grin leaking out of his violet mouth. The woman, before leaving, repeated the final part of her speech: "Glamorous, opulent, ornate doors before your eyes, forced right open, my masked young Judas, an Iscariot, lurking insidiously here, ancient verses, engaged to order. Luxurious door, you opened up eleven verse eight, revealed youthful treason, hiding inside nowhere, ghosts!"

On the tape, there was a long pause before the second interview, which was peaceful and short. The man must have been around fifty years old; he was wearing a dirty blue threadbare suit, and on his neck danced the greasy tassel of his hair, which he combed over his forehead to disguise his baldness. His hands were clasped in front, as if he had just taken off a hat and was holding it there, and, as he sat down, he placed them on the table with his palms facing each other.

I asked him the same questions, phrases that he listened to attentively, repeating them syllable by syllable, in an agitated whisper, muted as an echo. His initial responses sounded empty and irrelevant. But suddenly he stuck out a finger like a pencil, sliding it on the desktop, and drew arcs and straight lines on the dusty surface. He was writing, and when he had advanced enough with those letters that no one else could see, he stopped to read them, this time with the sweet and false voice of a priest giving mass: "That's what Daniel told me. In a certain place there's a man and women three, that's what there is. What else could there be? That night and every night. You've got to reduce the factors, don't get distracted, reduce. That's what Daniel suggested. So in a certain place there's a man and women three, and what else could there be? A man and a triad, a trinity, a triumvirate, a triangle, a tripod, a trilogy, a tricycle, a triplet, a trio of women. Does that ring a bell? That's what Daniel asked me. And this is what he said, in a

certain place there's a man and women three. They have a history.
I was just a kid, a calf, a colt and I had three women. One was
my fiancée, another my lover, the other my sister. None was my
mother; my mother wasn't there. That's what Daniel told me.
And my lover disappeared and existed nevermore, and my fiancée
disappeared and existed nevermore, and my sister disappeared and
existed nevermore. In that order. Does that ring a bell? That's what
Daniel asked me. One is an instrument. I have not killed anyone,
I've never meant to kill anyone. That I did not see. This is what
Daniel told me."

The rest of my questions obtained the same response. I listened
to the recording closely, scouring it for some difference that might
express the poor man's desire to alter his speech, but there was
none, they were only the same words in the same sequence, with
identical pauses, a prison that he had constructed around himself
and from which he did not think to escape.

Vicario took the patient by the arm and led him toward the
hallway. A moment later he returned with the third. She was a
woman about thirty or thirty-five years old. A diagonal scar traversed her mouth from a nostril to the tip of her chin, surely the
correction of a leprous lip. Her eyes, almost always half-closed,
trembled beneath their lids, and she would open them every
once in a while to reveal one black pupil and one covered by a
dark, dense cataract. With her, there was not even the faintest
hint of a conversation. Barely had she heard my voice when she
plunged into an infinite enumeration of dates and names, a long
psalmody that began with a fragmented story and continued
with a roster of foreign surnames, a chant that would vanish for
moments and return all the stronger, like a mantra. And as she
recited this, she paced from one end of the room to the other,
stopping to face a wall, far from me, or coming up close to

breathe her fetid, saccharine breath in my face. In the café that night, I tried to transcribe that infinite list on paper, until the chore made me feel ridiculous.

I managed to copy down the first few phrases: "According to Conrad Lycosthenes' wife, who was a foreigner, the women of her country used to lay eggs like hens. Conrad killed her and on her deathbed found a yellow egg and through a crack in the shell saw a sleeping face that was identical to his own. Ramihrdus of Cambrai was born of a virgin hen and they killed him: 1076. Gherardo Segarelli preached to the wise men in the barn and they killed him: 1300. Fra Dolcino bred chickens and roosters and they killed him: 1307. Jan Hus made Peter sing thrice and they killed him: 1415. Jacob Hutter disemboweled his disciples and they killed him: 1536. Anne Askew quenched the thirst of her chicks with her own blood and they killed her: 1546. Nicholas Ridley's feathers were plucked for being the king of the Jews and they killed him: 1555 . . ."

Dozens of names. The woman went on to lower her voice little by little, until it was transformed into a buzz, and the nurse put her at ease by rubbing her shoulders as she led her out of the office.

Vicario looked at me with amused eyes and said, "So then, according to your friend, these are the *reasonable* kooks, right? These ones were going to get him out of the darkness? Eh?" He rubbed both sides of his face with his thumb and middle finger, stifling the hiccup of another cackle, and he added, "If you find anything worthwhile in all this, I'll hand over my house and give you my wife, Mister *Psycho*-linguist. For now, leave me in peace—go ahead and take those documents and bring them back tomorrow, but, please, I want to rest. If I can manage to spend a few days here, staring at the ceiling or pretending to investigate, I'll free myself from walking around the office or on the street, from running unnecessary risks, see what I mean? Get out of here. Take your recorder and do me the favor of turning off the light on your way out."

I did as he said, and before leaving, I pulled the rusty chain of the fluorescent light. When the darkness returned, the white streak of the window bounced over the desk, on Vicario's back, in the mirror, and projected the profile of his nonexistent partner, composed of reflections.

I took off the headphones, turned off the recorder, left some money on the table to cover my tab, and exited the Halfmoon Café, waving goodbye to the anorexic twin while her sister cleaned the tables in the back. I never want to get home, but that night I had too many questions running through my mind, and I knew I would be able to clear up at least one of them if among my wife's boxes I could find the enormous black Bible that was given to us as a gift from her mother one thousand years ago. The first woman had cited a verse from Zechariah. "Benevolent Zechariah," she had said. "Eleven verse eight." I quickly scoured the Book of Zechariah for verse eight of chapter eleven. And the quote, according to the woman, was "Benevolent Zechariah blessed my uterus in felicity, sorority, fraternity." One need not be a theologian or even a believer to notice the apocryphal ring of the phrase. I unearthed the boxes from a closet, and among albums that I preferred not to look at and packets of photographs that had begun to yellow, I found what I was looking for. Zechariah 11:8, as I confirmed, said nothing similar to the quote the woman gave. What it does say is this: *In three months I made three shepherds die and my soul loathed them, and their soul also abhorred me.* A hunch sent me running for the woman's patient history, until I found the diagnosis I was expecting to discover: chronic severe echolalia.

The woman would repeat literally any text she was given to read, until someone put another text in front of her eyes. She was incapable of participating in a dialogue, and "answered" questions with fragments of the most recent text she had learned. I searched through the histories of the other two patients and found the same behavior. I realized that Daniel had not asked me to interview these patients because they might have witnessed, seen, or heard something, much less that they were guilty of anything. What he had done was send me three messengers. Why had he encrypted them? To stop Vicario from understanding them, if he were present during the interviews, as indeed he had been? And why send me messages that were days old, and run the risk that I might not understand anything, rather than telling me everything I needed to know during our previous conversations? That was another story, and it would have to be revealed to me at another time. In the meanwhile, I had two pending tasks for the rest of the night: go to the meeting with the young man from the Biblio Path, and, after that, submerge myself once again in those apparently meaningless transcriptions in order to discover if they were, as I was beginning to suspect, chapters of a sinister confession.

The Antiquarian reads: There is a triangular village, presided over by a church of mud and cane, with the entranceway of steps sunken into the skirt of the mountain. The village occupies the narrowest pass of the valley, and it's an obligatory route for travelers and rustlers, and on Sundays, the point of confluence for the lonely people who inhabit nearby hills and plateaus. On a certain afternoon, from the end of one of the three streets, a group of strangers appears, some on foot, others on mule or horseback. They ask for the authority figure and an old man comes: my name is Abraham, he tells them, his forehead scratched, his corneas yellow. They make him call his son and the man obeys. Isaac! he shouts, or maybe, Ishmael! A boy comes running from the shadow of a straw broom, with a hen in his hands, and thus the judgment begins and the father's crimes are stated aloud in the plaza: rewriting the law, redrawing the borders of the land, reconciling faith with desperation. A tribunal of adulterers and thieves finds him guilty. Then the strangers turn toward Isaac, or Ishmael: you must kill your father, they tell him, a lesson for everyone to learn from. They place a rifle in his hands, and when they leave, on foot or mule or horseback, picking up the path on which they had arrived, without revealing the moral, the residents bury Abraham. The cemetery is so large that it encroaches on the streets and houses; new tombs are dug beneath the beds of the living, such that the bodies have only to fall down the stairs when they die. He doubts the reality of it: captivating, and yet, useless, the Antiquarian thinks. And he immediately decides to show Juliana that the spiral street, when walked in the opposite direction, uncoils toward an exterior loop of the city, where the houses are white and couples sleep together without exchanging garments or money. He takes her to live in the tower, unfolds before her eyes rolls of canvases with anthropometric calculations, lines of references written in cursive, upon human shapes in impractical positions.

He extracts from trunks and sideboards miniature volumes of fantasy or naturalist tales, and placing a clock-maker's cap on his head, he reads her one of these: wanting to leave the circus, behind whose doors he has always earned a living, the oriental beggar arrives on the shores of a meridional nation, and thieving the clothes of a public official, passes as a wise man, is transformed into an autocrat, and decrees the end of history, abolition of desire, and revolution in cathedrals and brothels, and he dies an old man, his hand stuck to the edge of a large cradle, without knowing that the buildings of his government are made of cardboard and that he had never crossed the threshold of the circus. Juliana looks at the Antiquarian, her shoulders, cheeks, and fingers clinging to each word, and asks for more, and between them an exchange begins—she showing him the virtues of a life among other people; he building the order of syllogisms and sentences learned from his books, elephant folios, imperial quartos, bound with paper, parchment, and Valencian calf—half the day in the library, the other half in the bedroom, one on top of the other, the eleven happy months of the Antiquarian's life.

NINETEEN

"The place you're heading, isn't it the Police Headquarters?"

"That it is."

"Are you going to turn yourself in?"

"That wouldn't be a bad idea."

When night falls, the air in the streets downtown acquires the oily consistency of a tank of dead fish. Breathing it is like ingesting a handful of wet clay through the mouth and nose, and to look at the couples who cluster in the doorways of bars and the secret meeting places of hookers and pimps and drug dealers in the glow of traffic lights is like seeing visitors at a zoo from inside a cage: their forms weaken and the contours of their bodies merge into a single mass of volatile, dubious matter. Insofar as one traverses the seven blocks of that diagonal street that originates in the first curve of the Biblio Path, one will discover strange gates, illuminated by cylinders of light that fall upon the sidewalks as if they were heavy, malleable objects, and in their suspicious glow, silhouettes of unhappy women and woeful men crisscross paths and form a simple volume of dusty, liquid, limitless phosphorescence. Mikrokosmos is no different—a black glass door under the engraved arc of a colonial house, an anthill of drunkards at the entrance, and, in the narrow hallway leading inside, a herd of circumspect youngsters, with mugs or bottles in their hands and ecstatic faces that express no real emotion. The spastic booming of the music makes the quincha composite walls shake, along with the wooden and marble floors, which you can feel vibrate in your body like uppercuts wielded by a ghost. Behind the bar there is a second cluster of little tables with plastic and aluminum stools. At the last of these tables I discovered the husky profile of the young man who had arranged the meeting. He had seen me from afar and had his hand raised to call my attention, and there was a pitcher of beer with two full glasses on the top of the circular table.

"I didn't think you'd come," he said when I sat down, and I didn't respond.

After a few seconds had passed, I said to him, "So, I don't have much time and I'm interested in hearing your story."

"It won't take long," he said, "but I want you to understand that I'm not doing this out of the goodness of my heart. You know what I mean?"

I had never paid for information before, and as I slid the bills across the green plastic tabletop, I felt for the first time that I was a fictional detective. He smiled visibly, the pinkish blemishes constellated in an arc of spotted stars on each of his cheeks.

He said, "I need you to tell me everything you know about Cabecita Negra."

I summarized, "I know that Yanaúma sells rare old books and is more illustrious than anyone else in that trade, that he used to have a real bookstore years ago and lost it in a terrorist attack. I know he has a certain inclination for mythomania and that he takes the stories of others and makes them his own. I also know that he was a friend of Daniel's and that he does business with his partners in The Circle and with many other important antiquarians in the city. I know he was Daniel's confidant, and that he knows the story of the other Juliana like the back of his hand—or at least, he seems to give that impression. And, given what you told me earlier, I know he hasn't told me half of the things that I need to know."

"Perfect," said the young man, slurping the mug of beer and wiping the corners of his mouth with two long, pointy fingers. "What do you know about Cabecita Negra and the trafficking of bodies?" he asked.

The ancient history that Daniel told me slowly came back to my memory. "I know something," I said. "That years ago Yanaúma was part of a group of book dealers who served as contacts between the employees of the morgue and the medical students of several universities. That they sold them human body parts to practice on and the sign by which their potential clientele could identify them was the monkey skull that used to hang from the awnings of their kiosks. I really don't know much more than that."

"Aren't you going to drink your beer?" the young man asked.

"I can't," I replied, and for some reason I felt obliged to explain. "The thing is, I take pills at night, and it's ill-advised."

"Good," he said, bunching together the pinkish blemishes on his cheeks again, "More for me."

"What do the body-traffickers have to do with this?" I asked.

"They have a lot to do with it," laughed the young man. "Yanaúma is still part of the trafficking ring. To tell the truth, he's the one who drives that entire operation. Ever since a minor incident with a journalist, they changed the sign. It's now a bust of Goethe that they place on top of their books. But it still works the same as it did before."

"And how is what you're telling me related to Daniel's story?" I asked, trying to skim the thin layer of foam off the top of my beer with the palm of my hand.

"Man, you still don't realize?"

"No," I said, impatiently.

"Well, I'm going to tell you without beating around the bush. My story doesn't have proper names because I don't know them, and I prefer to keep it that way, but I assure you it's the truth. One morning, over three years ago, your friend Daniel appeared in the Biblio Path. He always used to come, although for a while he'd been giving almost everyone the cold shoulder and would gravitate to Cabecita Negra's spot without paying attention to anyone else. Everyone knew him, as did I. He stood out from the other customers because he wouldn't browse through the stacks, as if those books had suddenly lost importance for him. Yanaúma used to wait for him with a minuscule package of two or three volumes wrapped in brown paper. But that morning was different. Cabecita Negra was not expecting him and was somewhat surprised. Your friend looked frazzled and nervous, and he asked Cabecita Negra to speak in private. However, I know exactly what they spoke of, though I'd rather not tell you how."

"Daniel had killed a woman. Juliana?" I asked. "His fiancée?"

"I don't know names," replied the young man, emptying the mug of beer only to grab the pitcher and fill it back up. "Daniel had killed the first woman and concocted a horrendous scheme to dispose of the body. That's what I'm going to tell you; that's what you've paid me for. Your friend devised a perfect solution, but he was unable to carry it out without the help of Cabecita Negra. This is how everything worked, this is what they agreed on. Daniel had the body in the trunk of his car for a day and a half, and then, perhaps that very night, he dumped it in a sewer drain on a quiet street not far from here. He didn't hide it or try to disguise it. He left it in a plastic bag, tied with a measuring tape, so that the early morning light would make it visible to the eyes of passersby. The idea was that the first neighbor would immediately alert the police, and this is what happened. Due to the jurisdiction of that district, the police, saddled with the routine of their daily diligence, were wont to take the body to the morgue where Yanaúma's associates

work—who, of course, had already been notified as to which cadaver they were to expect. They only had to push through some
minor paperwork and wait until the district attorney signed off
on a doctor's certificate saying it was the body of a Jane Doe who
had been killed with a sharp object, stabbed a certain number of
times, and additionally had considerable burns all over her body.
After that, only the date of the document needed to be changed,
pushing it forward two weeks, with the certainty that, as your
friend had promised, absolutely no one in the city was going to
worry over the woman's absence, and the police investigation,
without the pressure of any claimant, would be nothing more
than a bureaucratic drill."

"Is that how it happened?" I asked. "Did Yanaúma get his friends
to turn the girl's cadaver into an anonymous body and let her
decompose in the morgue only to return Daniel's peace of mind,
knowing that no one would take it upon himself to investigate?"
The young man smiled again. A dithering fly was walking along
the edge of his mug and from there leapt onto his hand and began
to climb up his forearm.

"It's not so simple," he said. "If your friend had only been waiting for that, he would've managed without the help of anyone else.
But he wanted to be completely in the clear. He didn't want there
to be any trace of her body and, more than anything, he wanted
to confirm that this had taken place, to see it disappear with his
own eyes. So the second phase of the plan commenced. During
the following two weeks, your friend came to Yanaúma's kiosk
each morning. From there, they took him in a car to a certain
house, and then to another, and someone would deliver to him a
part of the girl's body in a plastic box which he had to bring." The
young man spoke without any emphasis, putting forth a great effort to guzzle down the last large gulp of beer. The fly was walking

in circles on his arm, seemingly dazed, its minute wings mutely fluttering in the stentorian air of the tavern. Both of them were rubbing their hands together.

"One day they gave him a piece of the arm," the young man continued, "another day a femur with strands of hardened flesh still on it, one morning the liver, a kidney, a crosscut of the brain, a bag teeming with membranes, viscera, fingers and toes with the nails intact, the heart sliced in two. Finally, they delivered him the skin from the face and the cartilage still adhered to it, so that he could be sure no one was deceiving him. How was your friend making each part disappear? They didn't know. That was not part of their agreement. They only did what they had done dozens, hundreds of times over the years. Your friend paid them for each fragment, which they'd bring to him every day in a different part of the city, where he'd arrive blindfolded, as he had been during the journey there, and in a random taxicab he'd leave with his plastic container and some part of the girl's body inside, the ice from the morgue leaking into split bones and torn pieces of skin. But after the two weeks had passed and the delivery was complete, your friend returned to Cabecita Negra's with another similar story and the same offer of money in exchange for his help. Yanaúma argued with him—they were fighting, trying to disguise their agitation behind the little curtain of the kiosk which Cabecita Negra slid closed as the only means of privacy from the sellers and pedestrians on the Biblio Path.

"I saw that your friend was beside himself, sweating and all worked up; he seemed much older, suddenly deformed by the quaking of his hands and body, and when he left there he had an excessive sneer on his face and a nervous, involuntary grin on his mouth. Yanaúma had agreed to help him again, but something happened, something unforeseen, and your friend didn't return that time. Or ever again." The young man fell silent. He tipped the pitcher over the glass so that the last of the beer would trickle down. The fly took off. "I know what happened afterward," he said. "Daniel tried to kill himself and he couldn't. He confessed to the second murder and his father turned him in to the police."

The murmur of the speakers transformed into a slimy textured buzz devoid of any perceptible rhythm. A few couples lined up in the center of the bar, under the tubular neon green sign that formed the word *Mikrokosmos* in bent, soporific letters: men in cotton pants and worn-out shoes, women cinched at the waist who danced while staring at their feet or the reflections of others in the mirrors surrounding them. The young man's eyes were wide open, but he didn't seem to be looking at anything in particular.

"Well," I said. "I suppose that's everything."

"That's everything," he replied, still without looking me in the eyes.

"Thanks. So let me pay for the beer," I said. He didn't respond, and I placed another couple of bills on the table. "One more thing," I added. "May I ask you why you know so much about how that racket of body-traffickers operates?"

"Of course," he said, as he smiled once more, without raising his head. The sheaf of pinkish blackheads lining his lips framed the two strips of his dark, ulcerous gums. "I'm part of the ring. Why? Is there something I can help you with?"

TWENTY

I felt the urgent need to get home but, at the same time, a sort of vague terror about those four solitary, enemy walls, whose horror that night would undoubtedly be reinforced by the imminence of an atrocious discovery heaped upon all the others I had already encountered in such a short lapse of time. Now seated in the back of a taxi, I decided to delay the arrival of those secrets by walking part of the way home, and I asked the driver to drop me off at the beginning of the avenue that joins my house to the hospital. That dense mass in the shape of a coffin bore the appearance of a ruin from the future, the vestige of a tragedy that had happened a thousand times and, nonetheless, was to repeat itself once more, as soon as some overwhelmed god briefly turned his attention away from that world made of fragile columns and flimsy, foundationless floors. I walked with my back to the hospital, feeling on my shoulders the gaze of that building of minor mysteries and interwoven misfortune. A few blocks from there, the skinny twin of the Halfmoon Café was folding tablecloths and her stout counterpart was closing the place's metal gate with a crash. A drunkard was talking to a gray cat on a park bench under the streetlight. The wind was a flock of gaseous arrows in the liquid air of the night, and under that dry rain of dark tears Daniel's story was reproducing shred by shred in my mind.

Just as I knew, there was little to imagine. Daniel killed the two Julianas, with a fourteen-day interstice between one crime and the next. He devised a fantastic plot to get rid of the cadaver of the first, but killing the second one destroyed the defenses of his mind and led him to attempt suicide and then to confess to the second crime. But he kept the murder of the first woman secret from the police, in spite of the fact that he had revealed it to Yanaúma and Mireaux.

Was he also Huk's murderer? If he was, why so much effort to deny it and keep the first crime in the dark, if, as he himself said, his life could not be any more wretched? Why accept one crime and deny the others? And, more than anything else, why kill Huk? Could it simply be that Daniel was really a madman trapped forever in that stream of irrational violence, incapable of avoiding it, of lying, of stepping aside and letting it flow by without dragging him under it?

The doorman of my building was snoring under the cap covering his face, his legs outstretched in seeming discomfort on the reception desk. Instead of waking him up and taking the elevator, I decided to take the stairs. Few times have I walked up these stairs, especially this late into the night, and I was struck by their cleanliness, the tidiness of their checkered floor, the campaign of emptiness in this atmosphere that was so hospitable and, yet, for some indefinable reason, threatening and bellicose. The door to my apartment, the door to my refrigerator, the door to my medicine cabinet, where I searched for my pills, kept closing behind me without producing a sound. I left my office door open as I entered, and I placed on my desk the papers with the transcriptions of my interviews that afternoon with Captain Vicario and the three patient-messengers from Daniel. The utterance of the first woman had contained the signal that gave me reason for suspicion: the erroneous reference from the Book of Zechariah, which led me to the real fragment. *In three months I made three shepherds die and my soul loathed them, and their soul also abhorred me.*

Having already discarded my own questions and Vicario's interruptions, in view of the fact that there had been no grounds to suppose that they would have changed what the woman was going to say anyway, it was possible to build a composite text that had a certain, quite discreet coherence: "Yes, even still I know, now or what? The hours end fatally, inadvertently, and nobody cares enough, exactly over fire dangles another name, in eternal limbo. This here is silence, is sadness. This, his earnest knife edge you think hasn't a tang. Yes, our understanding aims recklessly, even looking on or knowing inside. Nothing goes forth openly, right? Now our window, a certainty. Hollow, anomalous, naked griffons, eternal pilgrims loom under some oblivion, never entering. Just go! Zechariah portends verdicts, maybe, possibly, perhaps, lunatic! God plays, smiling usward. Xenophobes play, queerly. Beasts! Mimic the zephyr! Placidly vaporize good Jehovah! Originate entirely cloistered from us sinners. Benevolent Zechariah blessed my uterus in felicity, sorority, fraternity! . . . Jehovah told peasants, old farmers, jailed outside, crucify! Flesh under Xanthippe's fire fears others. Glamorous, opulent, ornate doors before your eyes, forced right open, my masked young Judas, an Iscariot, lurking insidiously here, ancient verses, engaged to order. Luxurious door, you opened up eleven verse eight, revealed youthful treason, hiding inside nowhere, ghosts!"

If that, as I was suspecting, was a text spoken by Daniel to the woman, and if she was only repeating it, then I figured there must be some sort of invisible information behind the visible, as indicated by the mere words. The quotation from Zechariah had to be the sign, the front door.

I made three shepherds die was not much more than a transparent confession: three deaths. The two Julianas and Huk? But *I made three*

shepherds die is not the same as *I killed three shepherds*. It could be a
reference to an accomplice, to a hit man, someone who carried
out Daniel's orders, someone who acted by guessing or following
his plan or his instructions.

The light of my office flickered in a sandy bluster of wind that
blew in through the open window; outside, the sounds of someone
whistling on the street seemed to strangle the groan of a wounded
dog in the distance. What if the whole secret was hidden in the
Book of Zechariah? The Bible was still open to the same page. I
reread it for a lengthy period of time, sifting for overlapping signs
in the phrases of the book. Chapter eleven is dark and prophetic; its
hermetism rejected me phrase by phrase. In it, God is a merciless
entity, a killer whose acts are difficult to comprehend or justify.
He decides the death of the shepherds with the same animal facil-
ity with which he lets their sheep perish. *Let the dying die, and the
perishing perish. Let those who are left eat one another's flesh,* it says
after the quote that Daniel had wanted me to discover.

I read it again in vain. I could not find any meaning that
did not crack apart in bottomless speculations. I returned to
what the woman had said. After I read and reread it several
times, I remembered something. "Here even light lives on" was
a phrase that I had heard before, from the mouth of that same
person, the first day I visited the hospital. I reviewed the text
once more and discovered a second repeated phrase: "Glamorous, opulent, ornate doors before your eyes." But in that first
encounter, Daniel could not have already conjured up the plot
of those arcane messages. At least part of what the woman said,
then, must have come out of her own volition, had to be her
own words. Unfortunately for me, they were the least relevant
passages: "Here even light lives on" and "Glamorous, opulent,

ornate doors before your eyes." I found no meaning in them. A moment later, I remembered something else.

In our initial encounter, those had been her only words: the first ones she said as soon as she saw me, and the last ones, when I was walking away down the hallway. This time, too, she pronounced them at the beginning and the end. They must have been a formulaic greeting and salutation, spoken without any other intention than opening and closing the dialogue: hello and goodbye. So, I wrote *hello* and *goodbye* beneath those phrases and went to make myself a coffee. The kitchen was freezing and on the glass windows, opened wide, a translucent film of nocturnal dew had formed. In the park below, a policeman was making his rounds in the distance, and in the arched entranceway of the gates, vagabonds were loitering. I placed the cup on top of my copy of *The Purloined Letter,* by Poe, and when I turned back to the paper, a ridiculous correlation became self-evident: above the word *hello,* the phrase "Here even light lives on" revealed itself as the most infantile of acrostics—the first letter of each word formed the word *hello.* My laughter occasioned a violent and prickly bubble of bitter coffee in my throat. "Glamorous, opulent, ornate doors before your eyes" was *goodbye*. Perhaps all I needed to do was review the entire text as an acrostic—leave aside its contents and preserve solely the initial letters.

The following sentences said this: "Yes, even still I know, now or what? The hours end fatally, inadvertently, and nobody cares enough, exactly over fire dangles another name, in eternal limbo." Reducing the words to their initial letters, I formed the acronym: "Yes, I know. The fiancée of Daniel." Overwhelmed by a hazy enthusiasm, I did the same with the complete text: "This here is silence, is sadness. This, his earnest knife edge you think hasn't a tang. Yes, our understanding aims recklessly, even looking on or knowing inside. Nothing goes forth openly, right?" These words, which seemed to be, or perhaps were, scathing jeers directed at me, transformed into: "This is the key that you are looking for." The next fragment said: "Now our window, a certainty. Hollow, anomalous, naked griffons, eternal pilgrims loom under some oblivion, never entering." The lines hidden between the evident lines transformed into: "Now a change, plus one." I did the same with the next fraction and the result was inaccessible: "Jgzpvmpp-plgpsuxpqbmtz," then it said, "pvgjoecfusbzbm," and then "uifs-fjtpofjocfuxffo." But, from there on, the acrostic recovered its meaning: "Glamorous, opulent, ornate doors before your eyes, forced right open, my masked young Judas, an Iscariot, lurking insidiously here, ancient verses, engaged to order. Luxurious door, you opened up eleven verse eight, revealed youthful treason, hiding inside nowhere, ghosts!" was, according to my findings: "Goodbye, from my jail I have told you everything." Placing the results side by side, the complete paragraph was reduced to a notification with a new code embedded inside: "Yes, I know, the fiancée of Daniel. This is the key that you are looking for. Now a change. Plus one. Jgzpvmpplgpsuxpqbmtz pvgjoecfusbzbm uifsfjtpofjocfuxffo. Goodbye, from my jail I have told you everything."

Just before the three incomprehensible sequences, however, I understood that it had announced the variation. "Now a change. Plus one" must have been a self-referential phrase, one that I needed to understand in order to interpret those hermetic words. "Plus one: Just go! Zechariah portends verdicts, maybe, possibly, perhaps, lunatic! God plays, smiling usward. Xenophobes play, queerly. Beasts! Mimic the zephyr! Placidly vaporize good Jehovah! Originate entirely cloistered from us sinners. Benevolent Zechariah blessed my uterus in felicity, sorority, fraternity! . . . Jehovah told peasants, old farmers, jailed outside, crucify! Flesh under

Xanthippe's fire fears others. Glamorous, opulent, ornate doors before your eyes, forced right open, my masked young Judas, an Iscariot, lurking insidiously here, ancient verses, engaged to order. Luxurious door, you opened up eleven verse eight, revealed youthful treason, hiding inside nowhere, ghosts!"

The most direct route was to take the first letter of each word and search for the following letter in the alphabet. "Jgzpvmpplg-psuxpqbmtz," however, only transformed to "Khaqwnqqmhqtvy-qrcnua." Dead end. With a napkin I dried up the sticky puddle of coffee on the desk. Perhaps I needed to take not the subsequent letters, but the preceding ones. Rather than "plus one" in the sense of "add one," the woman could have said it in the sense of "I added one," as if dictating to me the explanation of an already completed event. I continued this reasonable path, and it bore fruits. "Jgz-pvmpplgpsuxpqbmtz," "pvgjoecfusbzbm," and "uifsfjtpofjocfuxffo" became a paragraph that produced a languid chill on my neck and back: "If you look for two pals you find betrayal. There is one in between." I couldn't stop my fingers from trembling and the coffee cup slipped, getting everything dirty with its lagoon of black water. I wanted to uncover the meaning of that phrase, but it too proved impractical. The two pals could have been, according to the previous line, the perpetrators of the crimes. Or perhaps Daniel was not pointing to the killers, but to his rescue plan which the young man from the Biblio Path had revealed to me that afternoon—perhaps the two pals were Yanaúma's contacts in the morgue.

From the beginning, I had suspected that the three messages Daniel transmitted to me through the three patients in the clinic were all going to be repetitions of the same confession, or reiterations of a single clue. But that might have been an error. They might not be duplications, I realized, but complements. It was clear that Daniel had not encrypted them in an extreme fashion, but rather only barely, only enough so that Vicario would not detect them, and in such a way that anyone with a paper and a pen could decipher them with ease. I decided to read the second text following the same method, but my resources were exhausted before they reached any accessible message.

"That's what Daniel told me," the subject had said. He mentioned a place and a man and three women, and grotesquely highlighted the importance of that fact: "a triad, a trinity, a triumvirate, a triangle, a tripod, a trilogy, a tricycle, a triplet, a trio of women. Does that ring a bell?"

Later on, his voice had been occupied by the voice of Daniel: "I was just a kid, a calf, a colt and I had three women. One was my fiancée, another my lover, the other my sister. None was my mother; my mother wasn't there."

It was not difficult to interpret, I thought: Daniel was talking about the two Julianas first, but then he was erasing Huk from the story and replacing her with Sofía, his little sister who had run away or been dead for so many years.

"And my lover disappeared and existed nevermore, and my fiancée disappeared and existed nevermore, and my sister disappeared and existed nevermore. In that order." The order he was alluding to, however, was transformed, in such a way that the death of the two Julianas seemed to occur prior to Sofía's disappearance. What could that mean? Was Daniel also responsible for what had happened to Sofía years ago? And the final phrase—"I have not killed anyone, I've never meant to kill anyone." Was this the denial of his guilt, or was it, rather, perhaps the latter part of the sentence, a nuance that ratified or excused the former, as if Daniel meant to say that by killing without wanting to, he was somehow innocent?

"If you look for two pals you find betrayal" was the most veiled line in the first woman's text. The two pals, then, could be Daniel and Sofía. The idea that he had involved his lost sister in the later throes of his luck and in the chaos of his madness seemed detestable, but I could not turn a blind eye to it.

Finally, I reasoned, Daniel could be unraveling something far more profound than the material history of his crimes: perhaps this was the revelation of a much more intimate case he'd spoken of so many times from the ledge of his soul. Perhaps Daniel was seeing Huk as the unfortunate replica of his sister: "The isles of terror where we used to live," he had repeated so many times, referring to himself and to the poor young woman. "Almost a girl," he had said.

One more text lay in store for me, that of the third patient, the woman with the mixed-up enumeration. "According to Conrad Lycosthenes' wife, who was a foreigner, the women of her country used to lay eggs like hens. Conrad killed her and on her deathbed found a yellow egg and through a crack in the shell saw a sleeping face that was identical to his own." From then on, her words were a roster of atrophied bereavements, names, distant dates, and a makeshift collection of slipshod histories. Conrad Lycosthenes, however, or so I learned by consulting my wife's *Encyclopaedia Britannica,* was a real person, a hemiplegic Alsatian theologian who had learned to write with his left hand after losing the ability to use his right. His most well-known work was a recapitulation of extraordinary events titled, *Prodigiorum ac ostentorum chronicon,* the unmatched catalogue of prophecies and supernatural omens that had inspired Nostradamus to write his populous manifesto about the future. In that eccentric reference, it was easy, to my melancholic surprise, to pick up on Daniel's bizarre sense of humor. I looked up the other names. Ramihrdus of Cambrai was a medieval apostate; Gherardo Segarelli, a millenarian preacher; Fra Dolcino (the only name that I was able to immediately recognize), a heresiarch inspired by Saint Francis of Assisi; Jan Hus, a Czech philosopher and reformer, worshipped in Prague as a national hero and with a host of followers to this day; Jacob Hutter, a hatmaker, Catholic by birth, but founder of Anabaptism, who had risen up from half-literate misery to the leadership of a church in the swamps of sixteenth-century Germany; Anne Askew, an Englishwoman who disbelieved in transubstantiation and preached against it, for which reason she was tortured as a heretic in the Tower of London, not long before Nicholas Ridley was found guilty of heretical blasphemies and, like her, was burned at the stake. Only when I noticed this similarity did I return to the previous names and discover that the coincidence was even greater: Ramihrdus, Segarelli, Dolcino, Hus, Hutter, Askew, Ridley—all of them, except for Conrad Lycosthenes—had died in the same fashion, reduced to ashes on a pyre due to the intransigence of their faith. The same occurred with the names that came afterward: Varaglia, López, Conte, Bruno, Coppino—all of them turned to smoke in the hearth.

The irregular stain of coffee seemed like the map of an island floating above the row of my papers, the edge of the pages darkened by the land of that continent buried in ground beans and half-diluted sugar. I got up to close the window, now that the wind was beginning to blow the curtains with a phantasmal howl and the sparks of a weakling mist were weeping crystal asterisks onto the desk. If Lycosthenes was a prophet, and the rest on the roster formed a succession of deaths by fire, what was the message that Daniel was sending me? Was he trying to tell me something about the past, or about the future?

I went to turn down my immense, deserted bed, where those questions would continue to gather and converge in the same insipid nightmare, which I dreamed, as always, without closing my eyes all night long.

The Antiquarian reads: A man has six sons, and one afternoon he takes them to church, climbing into the back of a truck. The wind, corrosive. The vehicle rumbles over the flat stones of the river. The chapel is a dollhouse deep in the woods. In the middle of mass two gunshots are heard, two cracks, two dry flashes in the air; the priest's forehead and his cassock are suddenly bloodstained, and when those present make their way outside, following the criminal's footsteps, no one is there. The trees, the expanse of the meadow, the silent countryside, the walls of the church painted in red, still fresh, with one single word, barely legible, repeated a thousand times on the bell tower: "Melencolia." Night falls.

On the hillside behind the church a sickle and hammer shine. On their way back home, the father asks each of his six sons, calling them by name: What did you see, Julio? I saw a man who was looking at me from inside a pond, his face attached to his skull with pins. And you, Guillermo, what did you see? I saw an island of mud melt into the sea, its inhabitants of mud melting into the island. And you, Mario? I saw a model of a green bordello set ablaze in the middle of the desert: night was falling and people were trapped inside it. And you, Gabriel? I saw the beginning and the end and the interminable succession of intermediate instants, and a mother breast-feeding her daughter and a drop of milk stopped still in the air. And you, José María? I saw a dog who was biting the corpse of its owner until finishing his flesh and I saw it bury the bones at the gates of Hell. And you, Jorge Luis, what did you see? I am blind, but I saw Juan, the absent brother, fleeing the church after killing the priest.

The Antiquarian leaves this book on the nightstand and sleeps next to Juliana, not long before dawn, when sleep has overcome them, covered them both in bedsheets of illustrated paper, intaglios, etchings, mezzotints that represent the same copper engraving: the figure of a winged man, at the door of a house on the seashore, a rabid dog at his feet, nails, saws, hammers, papers with emery dust, the plates of a scale tipping over his head, and behind him, the cautious tide and a bat that hovers in the sky with a sign hanging from his claws: "Melencolia." But later on the Antiquarian is woken by the tearing of paper and the rusty creak of the door closing. He sees that Juliana is not between the sheets, and he goes down from his high tower to the spiraling street, following her, trailing the flight of her dress around the corner, on the street that closes in upon itself, like the coiling of a serpent, where a crowd of shadows sits down with their feet in the road, eats in the doorway of the stores. He sees the hem of Juliana's dress slip behind the door of the house or the motel, and he goes up to the window, stays there silent and still, with his hands pressing on the glass, spends hours watching the movement of gazes, the fluttering of eyelashes and chattering of teeth, music without form or cadence that fills the innermost corners. He sees Juliana fall into the arms of a man, laughing, a bottle of liquor in one hand, the other slithering beneath a pant-leg. He sees her sitting on the lap of another man, lean back onto the chest of a third man, slip her tongue between the lips of yet another, climb back up the stairway taking one by the hand, until disappearing into the darkness. Overwhelmed, the Antiquarian walks the distance home, jumps up the final step, and, with his back to the bookshelf, lets his fingers trap a book at random. It is a dissection manual. The final pages depict calcographic figures from the seventeenth century, which artists used to fashion by placing a sheet of transparent paper onto parts of the human body, severed into slices, like pieces of ham: men and women seen from within, crosscut incisions, instructions for vivisections. He reads that book until sleep knocks him out. He lies down in bed, and when he wakes the following morning, Juliana has returned from her nocturnal saunter. She's asleep, her petite feet arched one on top of the other, like the hands of a newborn baby. The Antiquarian gives her a kiss on the forehead and goes to the library to finish his reading.

TWENTY-ONE

"Some straight roads don't lead anywhere."

"Some winding roads don't either."

Morning arrived as indecisively and slowly as a single unending cloud. I waited for it while scanning the path of a red spider next to the lamp. Surrounded by an invisible film of dew that sprinkled onto the pane, the window seemed to melt over the railing of the small balcony, and, through the kitchen's skylight, the rusty screech of the elevator's chains reached my ears, foretelling the arrival of another delayed, mechanical day. All night long I had debated with myself, and my decision was risky, and also, for the same reason, deadly. I was going to leave the resolution of my doubts in the hands of fate. With Vicario on one side, Daniel on the other, I was interested in talking to both, in order to get the captain to see my reasons for suspecting that Huk's death was a link in a longer chain of events, and that comprehending the nature of that crime was necessary in order to try to avoid an even greater one. Yet, what I had to say would require him to let me speak to Daniel first. For I needed to tell Daniel that I understood he knew much more than his messages had revealed to me, that I was still unable to secure solid footing in the face of the swelling list of revelations; but I also wanted to let him know—it was imperative—that deep inside me, I was feeling guilty for not having supported him during the difficult years of his breakdown and that, if he needed to talk to someone, this time I would be there to listen, perhaps with hatred, perhaps with disgust, but present, and that counted for something. While I was drinking the last drops of coffee and getting ready to leave, I saw the old photograph of my wife on a table in the living room, nearly faded in its black silver frame, the image yellowed by the sun, reduced to a stain of violets and oxidized greens. I felt like I had not looked at it in centuries. It seemed impossible to me that the world could already have left that invariable figure so far behind, that cracked statue from a time less real and less callous.

At the hospital, a perfunctory hand directed me once again to the little stairway down to the basement, where that metal doorknob and fleshy cavity of a corridor materialized before my eyes, filled with the sweet breath of insecticide between those walls reflected by the mirror behind the desk that Vicario had sat at the day before. No one was there. I would need to wait. Outside the windows near the ceiling, a stampede of wandering heels was traversing the sidewalk at street level, and a sheet of greasy light unfolded onto the file cabinets filled with patient histories and forms discolored by time. Fifteen minutes passed, or maybe more. The sound of footsteps arose and dispersed in the hallway, leaving a low echo in a series of violently slammed doors. In the uterine warmth of the closed space, a fly kept ruthlessly charging against the window. Another fifteen minutes trickled by without any change. I decided to go out into the corridor and look for Vicario in the other rooms.

It was a grayish hallway with linoleum floors polished to a glossy brown, and on each of its sides were closed doors. I knocked on the first one, but heard no answer. I wanted to open it, as well as the others, but the wooden handles, swollen with moisture, were locked. Next to the stairway, there was another room. I walked toward it expecting the same result, but to my surprise, it opened inward. The room was similar to the other one, but without any furniture, and against the walls, cardboard boxes were piled on top of one another by the dozens, like a row of flowerless plots in a graveyard, reaching up to the ceiling where spiderwebs were hanging, with moth cocoons and larvae entangled in the little arms of gray thread. I took two steps inside, listening to the muffled drag of my shoes on the carpet. Everything was still. But an unusual breeze was blowing through the upper windows, slipping between the gaps of the frames, and the cocoons and spiderwebs were swaying to the gentle rhythm of that lullaby. On the boxes there were no names or marks. Due to their grim passivity, they reminded me, for just a second, of the metallic drawers of the morgue, with the slow, perceptible decay of the cadavers. The door suddenly closed behind me. There was movement in the corner.

I turned around without thinking, rotating on my heels and losing my balance, gripped by a childish fear. Alongside a heap of boxes, there was a woman: branches of black hair falling over her shoulders to her stomach, her head tilted downward, and her fingers jutting out from her hands like nightsticks. She was emitting a faint reptilian groan and wiggling her body from side to side, as if she too were being rocked by the breeze, another larva in that room of half-made beings. Only her head seemed to vibrate at a distinct velocity, to tremble in brief, fractional spasms, wobbling in all directions, as if her neck were a taut wire that supported various dissenting and onerous weights. When the door closed, the room had filled with shadows, and only a guillotine of blue morning light, penetrating through the Plexiglas slots, allowed me to see a portion of her body, congested with rags, skirts, shirts, multicolor sweaters, one on top of the other, a ball of fortuitous yarn, layered upon that back hunched forward. The woman, sitting with great difficulty upon a box, her legs hanging inches from the ground, appeared like a quiet dwarf or a beastly bird barricaded into a corner of its cage in a zoo of shadows. She touched her temple with her hand, then lowered it to the height of her ear and tilted her head sideways, as if trying to listen. Her attentive expression multiplied the building's silence. I perceived the terrified murmur of my breathing, as though it had not come from my own lungs. The air froze in my throat. The woman turned her head, tilting her face toward me: a dark splotch of hardened skin, an eye covered by a fallen, formless, swollen eyelid, globular like a carcinoma grown under the forehead; her other eye open, black, round, hard as an iron ball encrusted into her socket, her iris rigid in the center, aiming at me, with the jitters of a trigger-happy finger. The wheezing grumble of her voice, thin as zinc whiskers, fell over everything: a single vowel sliced by occlusive fits and prolonged lapses of stammering noise, a tragic hiccup that seemed to pronounce a word, like a cough, constructed with the remnants of long-abandoned equipment.

She cupped one hand with the other, and she let her only open eye fix itself upon me. A painful startle brought her off the box, her two feet joined at the ankles, her knees bent in front of her, her torso twisted to the right. She took a step in my direction and stayed in the ray of light. An aura of silver sprouted from her straw-colored hair, from her concave chest, her uneven arms. She was studying me, looking me over, as if seeing me were a recollection; her eye ran over me like the back of her hand. She took another laborious step sideways and backward, resting her hip on the door frame. The moaning ceased. She parted the iridized ribbons that had replaced her lips, making me think she wanted to say something, but she continued to reposition herself, opening her mouth with the sneer of a silent cackle, revealing two rows of teeth in an orifice stripped of gums—teeth that seemed to be nailed into her jaw like coral hooks, like splinters—and a tongue that was a black blotch of meat, dry yet shiny and firm as a charcoal briquette. Out of nowhere, she snapped her head forward at me, and in the grayish glow of the room I saw her featureless, amphibious face, her skin striated in parallel lines of withering flesh, her salamander smile infested with fangs and pustules of filthy cartilage.

She raised one hand to her face in order to hold up, with an outstretched finger, the boil of skin that was falling like a curtain over the other eye. It was a white sphere, milky inside, a blind sphere scored with purple veins, without any eyebrow or lashes, without anything but that thickness of hardened froth, pasty like snot smeared under the superciliary arch. I wanted to leave, but the woman was blocking the door. I staggered back, trying to get away from her, wedged myself in between the cardboard boxes piled against the wall. A childish panic possessed me, the fear one feels upon waking from a dream, a nightmare of falling into a bottomless well. I was overcome by the absurd fear that I had awakened an army of creatures garrisoned in those containers. The woman resumed the vegetative whistle of her wordless voice.

She squatted down and stuck her hand under her skirt, poking around with theatrical gestures, as if she were adjusting the diaper of a baby buried between her legs. I heard a door open and close in the hallway, and then footsteps drawing near. She completed her search and extracted an object from her skirt, which I could not see but already hated. The door opened as the woman was placing the object on the floor in front of her. Two voluminous nurses dressed in green entered the room and, without paying any attention to my presence, grabbed the woman by the arms and made her walk toward the hallway, caught between their opaque, bulky bodies.

Barely had they left than I heard Vicario's voice calling me by name. The door opened once again, and the silhouette of the captain was delineated in contrast to the light from outside. I saw a look of hunger and fatigue in his eyes. He was twirling a toothpick in the corner of his mouth and had a bundle of printed papers in his left hand.

"What are you doing over there?" he asked, letting a flicker of humor shine through his tone. "You look like you've just seen a ghost."

"No," I replied.

"Come with me," he added.

When he had set off in a hurry down the corridor, I went up to the spot where the woman had stood and, shadowed by the door, searched for the object she had left for me near the bottom of the boxes. My fingers found it: a curvy, spherical surface, covered in a veiny, detestable substance. I held it in my hand and raised it to the light. It was an egg—the white egg of a hen, with the shell cracked and a drop of colloidal mass just barely dripping through its fractured surface. I instinctively dropped it and it exploded on the rug, in the beam of light. Under the shards of shell on the floor, the amber sphere of yolk floated in the transparent pool of egg white, and there was a miniature, yellow rectangle, like the paper of a fortune cookie. I grabbed it and carried it into the corridor. My eyes read three words, drawn in the trembling handwriting of a child: *Don't believe anything*.

Without knowing what to think, I mechanically placed the rectangular piece of paper in my wallet, stuffing it behind my wife's passport photo. Vicario had slipped through the doorway of the other room and, when I entered, was already sitting at his desk.

"What's with that startled look on your face, Mister *Psycho-linguist?*" he said in an ambiguous voice, with unfinished words that syncopated their own echo. At first I did not respond. He yanked the little chain in the ceiling, and the walls of the cubicle seemed to dissolve into the white. After a pause that lasted a few seconds, we spoke at the same time. Signaling with my hand, I asked him to go ahead. He changed his question.

"Did you have a good time last night with the recordings of your friends?"

"Indeed I did," I replied. "I think I may have discovered something. I'm not sure, though, and I'd like to speak with Daniel."

"Something about the death of the girl?" he asked.

"No, not exactly, but perhaps."

"If it's nothing that's going to help with the case, I don't see what need there is for you to speak with your friend." Vicario yawned, visibly unaffected.

I remembered a pending question, something that I had thought of during the night. "Tell me, Captain," I said, "when they found the body of Huk——"

"Of whom?"

"Of Huk. That's what Daniel used to call her."

"Ah, okay, Huk."

"When they found her body," I said, "in the autopsy, they discovered inside her a sort of mass of semi-digested papers, which someone had made her swallow, surely to kill her, isn't that right?"

"Yes, that's right."

"Well," I added, "as far as I understand, there was also a paper that was almost intact, a sheet of paper, isn't that true?"

"That's correct," said Vicario. "There was one sheet among many, one that remained *almost* intact, probably the last one she was forced to swallow."

"Okay, so tell me, Captain, is there a way to know if anything was written on that paper? Was it a page from a book or from a notebook? Was it printed? Was it handwritten?"

Vicario leaned back in his chair, slouching his shoulders and torso in order to put his feet up on the desk. The crunching of the chair's metal wheels scratched the air with a shuddering shriek. "In my world," he said, "murder weapons have no meaning. They are weapons, not messages. That girl was killed by asphyxiation. The papers have no other meaning than that. They are like the hands of a strangler—I don't care if they're tattooed or not, I only care whose arms they belong to. The only thing I'd be interested in reading on those papers are the fingerprints; and we didn't find any."

"And what about me," I said. "Could I see that piece of paper?"

"As you imagine," said Vicario, "I don't have it here."

"I know," I replied. "But later, later today or tomorrow, could I see it?"

"You can see it if you promise to stop bothering me. I'll make you a photocopy myself. And, as for your friend, you still insist on speaking with him?"

"I have to talk to him, yes. There's something I must ask him," I said, and Captain Vicario reluctantly smiled.

TWENTY-TWO

In the middle of the courtyard of gravel and sand, two men were staring into each other's eyes with unwavering fixation. Had it not been for the impeccable posture of one of them, the taller of the two, it would have been impossible to discern the patient from the visitor. Their expressions were identical; their fright, equivalent. Behind them, a woman was carving unfinished letters into the trunk of the nearest tree, and a few steps farther an old man with a lifeless face and serene eyes was belting out lines of a dialogue that he carried on in complete solitude.

Daniel walked through the wide entrance that led to the dormitory hallway. Something about his face made it appear to have grown older in a matter of three days; his eyes, sunken into their sockets, excavated by black cylindrical rings, an absent gaze. The cruciform scar on his forehead looked like a drawing on a glossy, marble block, and his cheeks were taut with a sigh that he never released. He stopped eight or nine feet from me, with his hands stuck to the sides of his pants. I didn't know if I should walk toward him.

"I thought you'd take a few more days before you came back," he finally said, from a distance, without raising his voice, trusting the emptiness of the courtyard to deliver his words to me. I decided to avoid the preliminary small talk, which I was in no mood to have.

"You sent me three messages," I said. "I think I've decoded them, partially, but I'm not sure that I've understood them."

"I sent you many more," he replied, "some of them placed inside others."

"Right," I said, "and I don't know if I understand them."

"You know what you need to know," he said. "And, at this point, you may know other things."

"I know that you've deceived me from the beginning, and that, in a way, you lied to me for several years," I replied. The woman next to the tree emitted a low howl of anxiety and, with a stone, continued to carve letters angrily on top of the letters already engraved.

"For a long time," Daniel said, "I couldn't have lied to you, because you weren't here. Nor have I lied to you now. I've only wanted to postpone the truth for a few days, that's all, and give you some clues so that you discover it on time." He was speaking softly, without irritation, but in some way his calmness annoyed me. I felt as if I detested him.

"You killed two people," I said with rage, "or perhaps there were three, isn't that right? Are you going to say it once and for all or are you going to invent another story to deny everything again?"

"*I never meant to kill anyone,*" he replied. "Everything just happened, it's as simple as that, Gustavo, and I have no qualms in saying that I was more a witness than a criminal. I saw myself and remember doing the things you're accusing me of, but I find no fault in myself. Isn't that what they call being alienated? To feel strange even to one's own acts, to feel like you're a stranger in your own presence, as if you were forced to lock yourself up in someone else's mind, like a prisoner in the mind of a criminal? That's what I've felt all this time, for the last three years—that they've condemned and imprisoned me between the four walls of a cell, that I am that cell, and my confinement has the hands and face of a killer. I feel no guiltier than you, and I find nothing in me to link me to my own history. If that's madness, then call me mad. I can't think of any other self-defense."

He fell silent. For the first time in days, his face contained an emotion. He was biting the inner edge of his lips, provoking an arrhythmic quiver, while sucking his cheeks into his mouth.

"Adela was your lover," I said. "Adela or Juliana, I don't know what you used to call her, she was your lover. You took her to you fiancée's house and had her live there, the two of them in one place, mocking them both at once. You took that girl out of a whorehouse and made her your servant, and then you killed her when she rebelled before the infamy of the situation. How did you convince her to go, to accept that charity? Why did you do it?"

Daniel's eyes turned toward the center of the courtyard. The two men standing still continued to stare into each other's face, mutually, victims of a resignation emptied of all nuance.

"Is that what you think?" asked Daniel. "That I killed the girl because she wanted to leave me? Because she grew tired of a game? So then, according to you, I killed my fiancée because—"

"Because she discovered something," I interrupted, bowled over, no longer thinking about what I was saying. "You killed her to hide the previous crime, but it didn't work, you broke down, you couldn't keep going on like that. A guy from the Biblio Path told me that story. You asked Yanaúma to help you get rid of the cadaver. Yanaúma had already done it with the other Juliana, with Adela. Or maybe it wasn't your conscience, maybe you only reasoned that this time Yanaúma's contacts in the morgue wouldn't come through, that someone was sure to inquire, sooner or later, about this Juliana. She wasn't an outsider who had appeared out of thin air, she wasn't a woman displaced by the war, a nameless prostitute without an address, a living dead girl that no one would notice, unlike the other one. They were going to investigate this death, and you would be the primary suspect—no matter what. Perhaps you confessed because you saw it was impossible to hide anything. Foreseeing that a major investigation would end up uncovering the first crime, you knew it would then be impossible to plead insanity, as you did, to put together that pantomime, which is transforming you into a real madman. When are you going to put an end to all this, Daniel?"

The fragile arms of the sun hid behind a wing tip of gray clouds; and on the other side of the closest bench the woman, facing away from us, scratched her writing made of cuts and splinters upon the tree trunk.

"The girl didn't want to leave me," Daniel said. "That's not how it was. We were different, the two of us. I was her confidant and she was my lover. I'd listen to her stories, the memories of that abstruse, distant war that only came to life on her lips. She'd give me what the other Juliana couldn't offer—pure life, the head of a body rescued from a shipwreck. Bodies are more alive when they have escaped death, Gustavo, that's what I learned from her. It was that involuntary love that effortlessly grew in her, and that she wore on her body like an outer layer of skin. She was a life-form unknown to me. I was going to say *wild,* but that's not it. Primitive, maybe, but in a sense that I was never able to explain. Or perhaps the word is *aboriginal;* with her I felt as if I were returning to the origin, to a beginning of which I had no memory, or a memory made of childish howls, prior to the source, to the uterus and to conception, something older than my life itself. No, she didn't have to leave me to make me feel that she wasn't mine. She never was. I was her public, her audience; it was my attention—not my body or my voice—that would fill her with life. When we were together, before and after sex, I used to feel guilty, when she would tell her story, when she would speak of the war. I would inevitably see myself in each one of those monsters that had molested her, raped her, wounded her, violated her, pushed her into the abyss. When the other Juliana was present, and the girl would feign the helplessness of a maid without any ties to me other than her salary and her conviction to please her employers' most minute whims, I would recognize in her the muted ferocity of her survival instinct. She was a person much more alive and real than any other, because she had learned that the world was an enemy and she had to deceive it at all cost. That brought me close to her, but, in the long run, it also led me to reject her. Her distance defeated me; it hurt to know that she didn't need me as a man, as a person, but solely as an audience, as a screen on which she could see her own reflection, or as the effect of the image of her life reflected onto the life of someone else. Her only weakness was a secret. She had to repeat her story day after day, to keep exorcising from her memory the backlog of suffering she had reconstituted cyclically, for years, in her remembrances, in her survival habits, in her penchant for taking on fake names, in the cruelty of not belonging anywhere, to any family, to any home, of not having ties to bind her to anything, but only masks, makeup, smiles that were lies told as loud as she could tell them. She never wanted to leave me, because she needed me to listen to her, but she wasn't with me either. She would move around within a defensive world made up of appearances, costumes, and shams. And she needed the world to be boundless. Nothing was enough to fill that void, and I least of all. She required new men and women around her, racket and shouts at every instant, a carnival of social climbers who'd enter and leave without a trace, a stain that would cover that other indelible stain, her past. She needed to constantly forget herself, in order to keep from remembering, in order to assume a character, and when her memory would besiege her, would corral her into a corner, on any given morning, on any given night, only then would my presence be essential to her, a reprieve, but nothing else. I only watched her and listened: In this I wasn't anything more than a spectator either, more or less distant, more or less secondary. The other Juliana was an anchor, a road sign, a house with locked doors, a future made of schedules, a first and last name embroidered onto the great white sheet of my existence. This Juliana, on the other hand, was a full theater, an entire spectacle. You can love a spectacle, but it will never love you back, nor will it even know you're there."

It was verging on noon. The friendly nurses were walking through the garden making their rounds. One went up to the couple of men standing still and said something to the taller of the two, who finally stretched out an arm and put it around the shoulder of the other, in order to lead him inside. An old, thin nurse in a green uniform approached the woman next to the tree and informed her that it was time for lunch. The woman looked at her with intrigue and circumspection.

"What did Huk have to do with all this?" I asked, again observing the deep rings around Daniel's eyes, even though I didn't want to and bemoaned my decision to look.

"Nothing," he said. "I already swore to you that I had nothing but pity for that poor girl. I don't know what happened to her, and, to tell the truth, I don't know if I even really want to find out."

"In the messages that you sent me," I said, "you don't mention her, but you do talk about Sofía." Daniel looked upward, far beyond the walls of the courtyard, beyond us and our conversation.

"Sofía *always* has been behind everything. From the day they went to look for her in the children's home and found nothing but a note and the little paper house, Sofía has been in my life, more so now than ever. Whatever I do or have done, whatever I think of doing or am about to do, is linked to Sofía. You don't lose a sister like you lose an ordinary object. If a sister disappears into thin air, that air is all you breathe for the rest of your life. I can't tell you anything else, but I ask that you believe just one thing. Soon you'll know everything, because I want you to know. But it's not time yet; I need a couple more days. For now, you are my audience, the only one I've got, and the only friend I have left. You may not feel like you are, and that saddens me, but it's true. And in a certain way, the things that you will know moving forward, I've already told you, yesterday, in the voices that you heard during the interviews."

The Antiquarian reads: A community rests between two mountain ranges, at thirteen thousand feet of altitude, in the frigid air. Five hundred people clustered in two rows of houses, or in crumbling shanties scattered across the mountainside, a permanent swarm of travelers and shepherds. Two unknown armies wage a war on the outskirts; they enter and leave the town on the way to battle, or to fall into ambushes, and the residents of the area start disappearing, siding with one or the other of the armies, or escaping with their kids on their backs, their animals slaughtered, their fields turned to smoke, or morning comes and they are chopped up and dumped in holes that start replacing the grass and fields. One day, ten men appear at the doors of a nearby cove—one of them is from the area, another is a face that's been seen once before, the other eight are strangers—and the townsfolk question them, take them to the hamlet. What army do they belong to? What kind of enemy? Why keep hearing their pleas instead of just tearing them to pieces and ending the threat? They kill the eight unknown men. They were journalists covering the war, but how were they supposed to know? And as night falls, they kill the other two, allies or spies perhaps, or maybe not. With the help of jars and bottles of liquor, they muster up enough energy to drag the bodies to a pit, don't startle over the sliced flesh, the extremities deformed from the blows, don't suffer for the victims who, in the end, will not be able to victimize again. In the following months, one hundred thirty-four residents of the town are going to die similar deaths, the killers will come from the two armies: the first explosion foreshadows the following ones, the place is emptied of people and eventually goes extinct. The last man from the town leaves on a crisp morning, headed anywhere, dragging four bags of clothes, crosses, pots and pans, clinking and bouncing between the stones on the path. He walks down between the plantations and valleys, endures freezes and downpours of moist grain and limestone, and one day he finds himself at the gates of the city. People look at him—he's different, speaks another way, his curved fingernails stuck into the cuticles of his fingers. He reaches the entrance of a street that closes in upon itself, like the coiling of a serpent, and, frightened, he walks along it. This is what I've come for? What kind of hell have I reached? Why didn't I just stay? he keeps saying, and that night he sleeps on the street, is going to sleep on the street for a long time, years, and the last thing he sees before sleep overtakes him is the profile of a man dressed like a raven, a book in his hand, a dissection manual, saving a page with his finger. He falls asleep and the man walks up to him, around him, thinks of tossing him some change, but doesn't, there's no time for that. The Antiquarian has other things to do. He has spent too many nights doing the same thing: waking up to find the other side of the bed deserted, walking down that street, invaded by strangers, toward the house or toward the motel, and there, leaning against the window, witnessing Juliana's descent into that abyss where each body is not met by another body, but rather by many bodies, seeing Juliana fall into a chain of hands that take turns squeezing her breasts, fondling her waist, carrying her into the penumbra of the second floor, returning, going up there again. The Antiquarian has meditated on all this, in the tranquillity of the tower, has rummaged through his book in search of an answer, risking his sanity in the quest, has promised himself that he will separate from her peacefully, or win her over with inescapable demonstrations, arguments, axioms, if he is only able to find them in the volumes of his library. He has laboriously scrambled from one tome to the next, always finding that the certain logic of his books does not fit with the macabre happiness of Juliana's smile. The world is made of binaries, there is harmony between like objects and harmony between opposites, and like objects repel each other and opposites repel each other. This is the reign of the universe, not any other way, no one has the right to de-calibrate that order, between two bodies, a border, between Juliana and him, only a border, a line, a limit; and yet not always, they have sometimes been only one. He knows this well—the world is made of oppositions, and opposition is the third element; once opposition is overcome, everything is one. Juliana walks around, arms crossed, opens her mouth, a carnivorous woman, a destroyer; the window is the border, an object on this side. It's me, Daniel, the Antiquarian, on the other side the profusion of sweat, tears, sleep, saliva, the litany of cries, the signs of disequilibrium. How can the order of things be restored? Juliana must evaporate into thin air. She hasn't betrayed me, she has undermined the principle of peace, and the Antiquarian sets off on his way home shocked by the clarity of his ideas. From the cabinet behind the bookcase of theology manuals, he removes the little case with the scalpel and the tweezers, the forceps and the disposable little wipes, everything so innocuous, so curative, and he readies the things with dexterity, filling out a form whose immediate authorization he has just written in his mind. In the following minutes, he will wait for Juliana to arrive, lying on the bed, covered with folded tissue paper, the dissection manual open on the nightstand, a copper lamp and parchment shade lit in the corner behind the commode, will listen to her come up the stairs, drunk, and undress, will pretend to get up, violently sleepwalking, will tell her he can't sleep and for the first time will open the car door for her, will turn the steering wheel in the opposite direction for the first time, escaping, that's what he'll believe, from the spiral street that closes in upon itself, like the coiling of a serpent, he'll leave the city and stop the vehicle next to a cliff, the sea below, the musk of shells at the shore. The Antiquarian will look at Juliana alive for the last time, pull out the scalpel, sheathed in the waist of his pants, and will approach her.

TWENTY-THREE

"Well, here we are."

"We're still two blocks away."

"This is as close as I get to the long arm of the law."

The Police Headquarters is a tall, diffuse building, a somnambulant Gulliver beached in the middle of an intersection where two streets meet with gray mouths and convergent lanes. A cloud of gannets surrounds it, soaring between electric wires and telephone lines, swarming in leaden flocks of oscillating points, and buzzards perch on the ledges of windows covered with iron bars and balusters, splitting apart from years of oxidation. When seen from the plaza, the building looks like a dried-out tree, on the verge of crashing down onto the avenue. Inside, the place is a maze of irregular desks, filing cabinets, and bulging plywood bookcases; through the hallways, thick with smog, a noisy procession of uniformed guards shuffles about, detectives dressed undercover and secretaries with boorish faces and shriveled expressions. Behind the tangle of offices on the first floor there is a bustling cafeteria crammed with blue-suited officers, sitting at the three tables in the back, and their defensive subordinates, who form a row of shaggy sheep, split into dozens of groups of starving guests, who grab off the counter disposable plates, plastic cups, monotonous servings of rice and murky beans and metallic little wells of thick salty-smelling soup with a skin of solidified grease on the surface. I looked at it and thought, That must be made of human body parts.

While I was staring at it, Vicario had come up behind me and put his hand on my shoulder, striking me with inexplicable alarm.

"Mister *Psycho*-linguist," he said. "Each time I run into you, your face looks more amusing." With the back of his hand eaten away by psoriasis, he wiped a red drop of something from the corner of his mouth and then crumbled a napkin between his fingers, throwing it into a wastepaper basket without first taking aim.

"I followed him up a spiral staircase, which creaked at each step, and then up another one, until we reached a den of diagonal walls with a window protruding over the avenue—a black ocean of churning waters, stirred in flowing streams, minuscule beings walking like lab rats.

"I have what I offered you," Vicario said. "However, helping one's neighbor without compensation goes against my most elemental principles. I can't show you the sheet of paper that the forensic specialists found in the girl's mouth, but I can give you a copy. Here you go."

"Thanks," I said, reaching out my hand to grab the paper. "I spoke with Daniel this morning, as you know. He insists that he had nothing to do with Huk's death, and he says that he's not even interested in finding out the truth."

"Well, if your friend chooses not to defend himself, it's going to be very difficult for him to save himself. He is the only suspect. And even though it sounds ridiculous, there's no one else in the hospital that could've had access to the 'murder weapon,'" he said, stretching out the sores on his cheeks in a bureaucratic smile.

"What do you mean?" I asked.

"That girl was suffocated," Vicario said, "isn't that right? Made to swallow pages and pages, thousands of them. According to the nurses, your friend had a collection of books in his room, a collection that, now, is simply not there. Like I said, it sounds absurd, but it's the only decent clue we have. And the fact that there's no one else in the ward with a criminal record. You know that your friend was found guilty of murder three years ago. That his internment in a psychiatric clinic is a systemic accident, or, at best, an oversight, but not an excuse. It doesn't mean he's any less guilty of that prior crime. Just by saying he doesn't know anything isn't going to get him out of another trial. And there's still the other sentence. His stay in the clinic can be revoked by another judge; it's not eternal salvation, it's just an accident."

I took the paper between my hands: they were two rectangles, reduced on the photocopy, surely the front and back, but the second one was blank, except for a small footer and a number in the lower right corner. It was easy to recognize the edge of the original paper toward one side of the copy; perhaps it was a facsimile reproduction from a book in octavo, or of a manuscript painstakingly copied. It was true: who other than Daniel could have had something like this in the hospital. I masked my concern and preferred not to read the words. Not yet. In the avenue, down below, an entourage of minibuses was knotting up in a jolt of honking horns and screams, and a pack of street animals pursued pedestrians on the brown steppe of the park.

"So then," said Vicario, "there isn't much you can do for your friend, just see him entangle himself in his lies over the course of the next few weeks. I imagine that, after this, you'll be off the scene, right? You're done playing detective? Nothing more for you to do here . . . Let justice run its course. You might get a bit of a kick out of that paper, but, please, if you find something, I ask that you don't come tell me about it."

On the way back home, I stopped at the Halfmoon. A fat hand placed a cup of coffee on my table. The paltry twin was watering the ferns in the flower box next to the front door, singing a monotonous song made up of whistling bars and codas. I placed the sheet of paper next to the cup. What had seemed to me like a series of handwritten words was really a succession of fonts broken and turned asunder by the imprecision of the photocopy. With difficulty, I discovered what my gut had told me to wait for. It was a passage I had just read for myself the night before. *And Jehovah said unto me, Take unto thee yet the instruments of a foolish shepherd. For, lo, I will raise up a shepherd in the land, which shall not visit those that be lost, neither shall seek the young one, nor heal the mangled, nor feed the one who be worn: but he shall eat the flesh of the fat, and tear their claws in pieces . . ."* It was the end of the Book of Zechariah. One word had been furiously underlined several times: *mangled*. Daniel had already cited Zechariah once before; this duplication was evidence against him. I pulled out my wallet, and next to the sheet of paper I placed the little yellow paper rectangle that the madwoman had left for me: *Don't believe anything*. Who was that woman? What kind of messenger was she? What kind of message was this? I regretted allowing myself to be led all day by my embarrassment in the face of the absurd, regretted not having asked Daniel if he was behind that nonsensical new clue too. Vicario said that I was playing detective, but I felt more like I was being played with by an army of hooded puppeteers.

"Do you have cigarettes?" I asked, without raising my eyes, focusing on the shadow of one of the sisters behind me, without knowing which one it was. A minute later, the box and the lighter appeared on my table. I hadn't smoked in years. The first drag transformed into a strand of scratchy air in my mouth. I felt its bitter flavor pass through my body, saw the white smoke curl out of my nostrils. *Mangled*. It wasn't a bad description of the madwoman who gave me that other message. I remembered: her heels split in two, her shinbones bent, one thigh crammed with goiters, the other, weak, with swollen veins, when she opened her legs to search between them. I remembered: the featureless face of a larva, the pointy teeth, the excoriation on her gums like peeled fruit, the tumorous appearance of shredded skin over her closed eye. I remembered: the gnomelike posture when she stood up, the straggling gait of those uneven legs, fractured and fused back together, the beastlike leap of her deformed footsteps when she moved through the hallway. *Don't believe anything.* Was *she* a message from Daniel? I remembered: the woman's gaze piercing me, as if waiting for me to recognize her, the hen's egg cracked on the carpet. I read: *the lost, the young, the mangled, the worn.* Suddenly, I understood. Or didn't understand. A surreptitious spark entered my head: the memory of a face, the day of a fire, a million years ago; a sinister intuition filtered through my bones, and I felt it slithering up my back, like a snake coiling around my ribs. I had to return home. I threw a few bills on the table and left running. I traversed the six blocks to my building with a whirlwind of ancient images pulsing through my mind: a red-hot ember rising through the checkerboard floor of the stairway; a cardboard house; forcing the key into the door; the mock-up of a tower being dragged among the bookcases, along with my hands, in search of a telephone book; the laughter of a girl digging her nails into the keypad; my voice asking if I could speak to Daniel, explaining I was his friend, that I'd just seen him that morning; a wall caving into the ball of flames in the fire while Daniel took an infinite amount of time to answer the phone. His voice faint on a line crackling with interference. Mine was terrified. "Daniel," I said, "this time it's serious. I need you to tell me what happened to Sofía."

TWENTY-FOUR

"Well done," said Daniel. "I didn't expect you to reach that question so quickly. I thought I'd have another day to finish the things I still need to take care of. I'll tell you everything." His words had the consistency of a nail pounded through the tip of a finger: solitary, stabbing, imperceptible; the telephone line transmitted them as if they were held up by columns of ice, like the dead body of a fish floating on the surface of an angry sea.

"I wanted to give you more time to understand," he said, "so that you could go on digging up the pieces of my history little by little. I thought that before tonight you'd have your reasons to doubt me, but then, later on, over time, you'd clear them up, unravel them, until you were finally left alone in the center with what has pained me so much to name: the Truth. I imagine that, in part, you intuited it. But you were there the day it all began, the day of the fire, the night when Sofía decided that our games had matured enough for her to take the leap from our fantasy mock-ups to real life, and she set fire to my parents' house, and to herself, and she stayed in the flames to observe the destruction of our house from inside it. *Home is where the hearth is,* do you remember? Sofía was never a common girl. Maybe that's why I was the only one in the house with whom she felt at ease, the only one she chose for the make-believe disasters she'd arrange with so much dedication, with so much unreasonableness, each time the loneliness and confinement of her immobility became insurmountable. She has always steered my life; her ghost is in every breath of my history, in every curve, every detour. In a certain way, Sofía died the night of the fire, but she is still with me. You saw her—an unbearable waste of the girl she had been before, deformed forever by the flames and by her disease.

"The things she used to say would startle me, and they'd frighten my parents too. That's why they preferred to get rid of her forever and stick her in a home for children, to erase her from our lives, rebuilding the house with one less room as a symbol of our amnesia. We pretended that no one else had ever been there. The night of the fire, you saw me, I entered the house frantically, with only one thought in my mind: save the library. All these years I've asked myself why I didn't think about Sofía, why I didn't wonder if she too was inside, if she was still alive, if I might have been able to do something to rescue her from the flames. Over time I've grown convinced that, indeed, I did have those thoughts—I had the guilty conviction that, somewhere in the house, the fire was destroying my sister, and I chose to ignore her. I ran between the ruins to save myself, collecting whatever books I could find, those books that were my life, without thinking about her life—but not entirely, and this is what hurts me the most, what hasn't let me live: I did think about her and preferred to ignore her. I entered, realized what I was doing, consumed by the ashes of the books, had the sensation that I was the one turning to ash and black soot on the bookshelves, and I went out without raising my voice even once to call to Sofía, without running into her bedroom, without knowing if she was still inside while I was escaping. That was the part of the story my parents could not understand. I felt responsible, and I had the feeling that, if Sofía was living year after year condemned among those breathless rag dolls in the children's home, shrunken among specters and buffoons, eaten away by the madness of an irrevocable imprisonment, it was all my fault. After several years had passed, I decided to do something about it.

"I wanted to convince my parents to bring Sofía back to us, to give her a room, hire caretakers, a permanent doctor if need be—to rebuild the world, I mean, to be a family again, to confront the darkest side of our lives instead of turning our backs. They paid me no attention. They had found a more comfortable formula: feigning indifference, even though that implausible pretension got lodged in their throats and chests every morning, every time they'd see an empty chair, every time a guest they hadn't seen in years would ask about the little girl of the house, and in their walks through the park, which they learned to avoid in order to refrain from seeing children on the streets, bawling in tantrums, squealing in joy. I didn't want to be part of that theater of shadows. *That's why I took her.* When they found Sofía's room empty in the children's home, the little note that she insisted on leaving, alongside the origami house she had demanded I build for her, my parents must have felt that her disappearance was the end of the tragedy, must have seen a benevolent omen therein, the sign that their lives could take a new course again—someone had saved them from the anxiety of their daughter's constant agony, from her troubled presence and its control of their lives at a distance, from a lost room in the labyrinth of a hospital masked as a home. That's why the investigation was spare and apathetic, minimal—to save face, so people would see them destroyed for a time, a few months. But deep down, they were more wretched than that, of course. They acted out one form of grief to hide another—they didn't mourn the loss of the girl, but the indifference with which that loss penetrated their hearts. They were longing for relief, and the kidnapping of my sister afforded them just that. So there you have it: I was the one who took Sofía.

"I had her with me for years; I've had her with me the whole time. I've watched her grow, break her bones one by one, I've seen her smile in response to the crackling of her joints tearing apart, I've had her in my arms each time her wounds got a new infection, during each week of hunger and anger. I've seen her become a nightmarish woman, how her madness has sprouted, and her obsessions too, which I learned to avoid. I've placed her in the hands of doctors and psychiatrists, I've been her nurse, I've fed her hand to mouth, I've cared for her dreams spoken in moos and clucks, I've been her father and mother. I've had to witness her conversion into a monster, the painful aphasias of her tongue, her habits of an aged girl, I've mentally multiplied her featureless face, I've seen mine in hers, devoured by the abjection of dementia, I've dreamed I was part of her body, listening to my ribs break and transform into fish skeletons on the beach, into the fuselage of broken airplanes, into a pile of garbage shredded by the small-est movement. The illness has ceased over time, but her body is a ball of deformities, and the madness has increased to the point of leaving no trace of humanity in her gaze. Sofía is an apparition, the vestige of a person, a dubious little animal that seems to entertain herself with mirrors, distinguishing the vagueness with which her features evoke the face of a human being. Her deformity somewhat amuses her; when she was younger, way back when, she used to subject me to the torture of her ecstatic expressions when one of her bones would break. She would celebrate it with a racket and would, sometimes, do it on purpose. The sickness was her favor-ite toy. Now, I have learned to expect horror when she changes moods, I know how to look out for the deceitfulness of her humor, to prevent the cascades of savage rage that subtly imprison her, prompted by even the slightest of triggers, or without any visible motive at all. I've learned her habit of unexpectedly escaping, and that has been our tragedy.

"More than three years ago I interned her in an asylum, not far from here, under a false name, as always. I presented the doctors with one of the clinical histories, which I now know how to counterfeit. They accepted her, though not without reservations. Her condition is not only mental, and her propensity for contracting illnesses without an apparent cause makes her a patient that few dare battle. At the time, I had already taken Juliana—I mean Adela—to work in my fiancée's house, and I was living that strange honeymoon that repulses you so deeply. Each day I'd go to her apartment and spend hours there, observing the conjunction of the two women, imagining that they were only one. On Sundays, I'd wait for Adela to return to her home so that I could pick her up, drive her to a motel, and spend hours listening to her stories, before and after losing myself in her body, plunging into the guilt her words awoke in me. One night, when I returned to my parents' house, Olga gave me a note with a phone message written on it that had surprised her: they were calling me from a hospital, regarding a woman whose name the maid didn't recognize. Of course, it was Sofía. I called the hospital and a doctor with a quivering voice told me that the patient had disappeared, a caretaker had passed through her room on his rounds and found no one there. They searched everywhere, he said, alerting the guards and running through all the hallways, lobbies, and rooms, to no avail. For a moment I thought it was a dream, that I'd wake up to discover that my guilty memory was playing a trick on me. But, no. Sofía had escaped and this time, I wasn't responsible. That Sunday, at Adela's house, I did nothing but gnaw at my conscience, methodically, boldly, judging myself again for the night of the fire and for the negligence and carelessness of my precautions. I had felt free of Sofía for a few days, I'd abandoned her once more, and this was her way of letting me know she resented it.

"That week, the two women divided before my eyes. Their bodies, which I had imagined as only one, were severed, amputated, revealing the delirium of my desires. The following Sunday I decided that, when I went to Adela's, I was going to suggest we break things off. I had to free her from servitude and free me from myself, and I'd tell this other Juliana that our relationship no longer made any sense. Adela would be waiting for me to arrive at noon. I knocked on the door several times without receiving an answer, and I finally turned the knob, but the door opened without my needing to push it. In the front hall was an overturned table, the pieces of a porcelain bird scattered among flowers and pools of water; at the foot of a changing screen I saw drops of blood, and on the stool next to the old sofa in the living room a dot of mud, purple as a scar. I found Adela's body in the bathroom, her legs draped inside the tub, her arms stretched down like the wings of a bird that had smashed into a window and fallen to the floor. Her naked torso was bitten by a double row of long thin wounds, like slots, crevices of foamy blood, nailed together, stitches of a bestial darning that sewed the skin against the skeleton; under her chest, in certain areas, her ribs were sticking through the skin like stabs inflicted from the inside. Her arms and legs had been burned and were two tumescent sticks colored gray, speckled with craters, a range of black rashes that ended on her hands and feet with transparent fingernails and toenails—the only thing that remained intact. The shower curtain and the little bath mat between her legs had been burned along with her, and the lagoon of dirty water on the floor contained an archipelago of caked ashes. I felt nauseous, started to gag violently and threw up a stream of yellow bile. I took a few steps out of the bathroom, dazed, dumbfounded, without knowing how to react. In the middle of the room, there was a little white origami house, with a red heart drawn on the door and four fingerprints marked in brown blood on the paper: I felt demented; I felt dreadfully mortal.

"The following morning I spoke with Yanaúma. That part of the story you already know. Can you imagine what comes next? Sofía, feeling my betrayal, spying deceit in my absence, feeling mocked, had killed Adela. She had followed me to her house, had discovered the plot of the two women, had felt that childish jealousy that a girl can feel for an older brother's girlfriends. She decided to put an end to them, teaching the only lesson she knew: the tests of fire that cure witchcraft, that release angels from the chests of magi, that make brave princes moan in desperation on starless nights, the tests of fire against evil and in favor of evil, the fire that purifies and estranges, that deprives and gives to full hands, the hearth where the tough turns tender, the raw well-done, before charring to a crisp. She killed Adela by stabbing her and lit her body on fire. *You don't light a pyre, but a labyrinth of fire,* isn't that how it goes? Do you remember the quote? *This has occurred and shall occur again.* It's from a play we staged many times, years ago, in our games at home. Two weeks later, Sofía killed the other Juliana. To assume the blame for that second murder was my way of vindicating myself from my sister, of cleansing the shame, even though I could never cleanse my guilt, and in spite of the fact that she would never understand. I found my fiancée dead on her bed. Sofía had pierced her body with a knife, she had burned her thighs with a hundred matches, which I found scattered over the body, and she had lit her hair on fire so that the face would swell up in the flames. Finally, she threw a bucket of water on Juliana so that her body wouldn't turn to carbon, to make sure I'd recognize her under the blisters.

"Beside myself, I looked for the white paper house and found nothing. I ran through the apartment, space by space, room after room, and in the shadow of a cupboard, wedged between boxes of preserves and cans of oil and milk, I discovered Sofía. She was looking at me with her wretched face of a punitive archangel. I wanted to ask Yanaúma to help me again. I did, and he denied me, but, anyway, I later realized that it was impossible, and probably useless. Someone would ask about Juliana, her friends would immediately notice her absence, the police would interrogate me. Would I be capable of hiding Sofía and at the same time alleging my own innocence? I was sure I wouldn't be able to. The police would need a culprit, so that they wouldn't keep snooping around and eventually find the only secret I was interested in keeping, the secret of my sister, the living corpse—my crazy sister. That's why I faked my suicide attempt, that's why I turned myself in. Before going through with it, however, I'd seen to it that Sofía wouldn't be left to the wolves. That same night I came to this hospital and pushed through the paperwork for her internment. *My sister is here,* under another identity, in the parallel ward, with her bills paid for many years. That's the reason why when my mother, who knows nothing about any of this, started to pull her strings with the judges, I insisted I be allowed to come to this place once my sentence was commuted. To know that she was close, to take care of her, to protect everyone else from her. But I never thought my mother would make the weight of her money go so far. She made sure I wouldn't even have to live in the ward with the dangerous patients, where, as per my own request, Sofía was placed. That's why I haven't been able to see her, though, as you can imagine, I'm well aware because of her actions that she's still around: she's the one who killed Huk. She choked her to the point of asphyxiation, stuffed her body full of pages from the books that I myself left in her room the morning I brought her here, the same day I faked my suicide attempt. When I entered Huk's room, the day they found her corpse, I saw the long bumpy wire that Sofía had used to stick those pages into her mouth, pushing them down to her stomach, letting the body, as the material continued downward, start to half digest them into a fantastic, milky bolus that the coroner discovered in the autopsy. I took the wire and hid it in my clothes. I also saw, upon the bed, the paper with the quote from Zechariah and the underlined verse. I had the intuition that it could be used to place blame on me once again. I read it, folded the page, and placed it in her mouth, where the tips of many other pages were poking out. That's how I went on piecing together the clues, that's why I got rid of my books, I looked for the messengers, and I called you, knowing you would immediately blame me, but calculating that you would also have to decode the truth in the long run, over the course of these weeks, in the jail of these repeated nights. I needed you to believe I was responsible for everything, and I also needed my innocence to appear clear to you. I trusted you, but not your swiftness, and that was another mistake of mine. Now you know what there is to know. Now I have nothing else to tell you, except for one thing. I ask you, in the name of our friendship, to keep this secret, which has cost me my life. I need your silence, at least for one more day, one more night."

Daniel hung up and I kept the telephone pressed against my ear for a long time, listening to the murmur of the void on the other end, and then the warble of the dead tone, which was invading my head like a call for help. Evening submitted to night in the rectangle of the window, and the silhouettes inside the houses were becoming crisper on the opposite side of the park. So there I stood, my eyes crippled, lost in the low clouds lurking over the trees, under the blurry trunk of that starless, birdless sky, devoid of any glimmer at all, in the opaque dome of the city.

I don't know how many hours went by while the night deleted solid bodies from the avenue, replaced the fences around the park with a ribbon of platinum fog that made the grass look like a pool of water, under the shimmering splendor of signs lit by floodlights, the only trace of artifice. Far off, several blocks away, a sphere of orange light radiated in the darkness, a stain, shifting like a medusa, spinning in the air and adopting multiple forms. It kept growing, transformed into a long red-branched flame with a column of smoke rising over it, blacker than the night sky shrouded with colorless clouds. It was a fire.

I ran down the stairs to the lobby and took the sidewalk that borders the park and opens up diagonally toward the hospital, walking in the direction of the fire. I was walking without haste, but agitated inside, nervous to discover what I was anticipating and terrified to see it with my own eyes. I did not need to go very far in order to confirm that what was burning was in fact the hospital, the long segment of thatch buried in an unfathomable fireball, which was spattering hysterically and wrapping everything in its labyrinth of fire. The wailing of fire engines was eclipsing the shouts of the patients, who were running down the road with the stupor of rare freedom reflected in their faces, their scarecrow-like figures slipping in the rain of filaments and splinters of blasted, pulverized wood and the drizzle of mud that cooked in the hovering dew and rising cloud of smoke. They were tumultuously galloping down the avenue, venting howls of surprise at that irreversible world that they were starting to take by storm, that they were invading and capturing, that world now tinged in black and red, an army of volatile gargoyles that scattered their groans into the night, spirits of rancor and duress set free by the fire, passengers in the flames of that final burn.

The outer ring of the hospital had collapsed inward under the weight of a fallen rooftop. Inexplicably, I walked through it, stepping on the rubble of toppled walls broken on the ground, and I advanced, far from myself, not opposing that blind long-fingered hand that was attracting me as in a hypnotic trance toward the inside of the building. I took a few steps into the courtyard of gravel and sand. The two trees were broken like bones, crouching down, as if fleeing from the flames, the ruins of the spiraling hallway deceased in a trail of hard lava, among stones, pebbles, reams of burning cardboard, and cushions that looked like flaming rib cages upon bases of shattered metal. And in the middle of the whirlwind of tremors, in the center of the corrosive spiral of black winds, currents, and miniature embers that began to fill my lungs, I saw Daniel, sitting on the ground, in an arbitrary spot of that nightmarish maze, and in his arms, stretched out in his arms, wrapped in Daniel's arms, a second before a burning beam came crashing down on me, I saw the woman, or that's what I think: *Don't believe anything.* The face of a featureless fish, her broken arms, her stiffened thighs, an eye closed up under a giant ball of flesh, the other eye open, relishing the spectacle, the final spectacle, in her dream of crazed pyrotechnics. The woman was Sofía. She was dying with her brother, in that interminable fire whose first flame had been lit, as in a children's game, an entire life ago.

The Antiquarian reads: In a certain country there is a war, a decade and a half of killings, sixty thousand people die, and everyone still living has a tragedy to tell. The criminals and the survivors go on losing their wits one after another, and soon the plazas of the main cities become camps where everyone, with feelings of perdition and the intuition of a night so long it barely ends, learns to tolerate one another's company again. A legion of wandering migrant masses organizes in that chaos of crammed sidewalks and streets, finds a different order, founds a populated country on the streets of one that's been deserted, and thus reunited, criminals and survivors agree upon a new law: no one must ever speak about the past. Some people find it impossible to comprehend this never written, barely uttered code. They are gathered one by one, and a hospital is opened for them, made up of two identical wards that have no contact with each other, each with a courtyard in the middle, the ground made of gravel and sand, and to the hospital, one by one, arrive two children who say they saw the feet of their lynched father fluttering in the air above them; an old man who swears to have perceived one night, some time ago, the bellows and gears of the legendary torture chamber and its rape machine; a boy with green teeth and tongue whose father, he says, has died and come back to life with thirty necks, sixty eyes, six hundred fingers; a young man called Isaac or Ishmael, who has killed Abraham in order to learn a lesson, but never received an explanation as to what it was; an old man whose six sons try to call the hair, hair, the tooth, tooth, the tail, tail, and not ever name the rat; the final inhabitant of a community of five hundred people, forty of whom, including him, one afternoon, killed eight journalists and then two friends, just in case, out of terror, and have themselves begun to die, without knowing why or for what; a very young woman who doesn't remember her name, a multicolored blanket over her shoulders, as if transporting on her back the weight of an

absent child, with one single word on her lips: Huk; and an Antiqua.
who has gone mad with love and loneliness and who, wanting to reinst.
order back into the world, in accordance with what he has learned i
his books, this day has gathered the other people around him, in a circle
composed of specters and lost souls, in the nonexistent shadow of a tree, to
tell them his story, to become one of them, and to escape.

ian
te
n

GUSTAVO FAVERÓN PATRIAU is the director of the Latin American Studies Program and an associate professor of Romance languages at Bowdoin College. He is the author of two books of theory and has edited anthologies on Roberto Bolaño and Peruvian literature. As a journalist and a literary and social critic, his articles and essays have appeared in publications in more than a dozen countries.

JOSEPH MULLIGAN has translated *Against Professional Secrets* by César Vallejo (Roof Books, 2011), and his translations of Sahrawi poetry appeared in *Poems for the Millennium Volume IV: The University of California Book of North African Poetry* (2013). Forthcoming works in translation include *Mawqif* by Pierre Joris (La Otra, 2014) co-translated to Spanish with Mario Domínguez Parra, as well as *Selected Writings of César Vallejo* (Wesleyan University Press, 2015). He resides in New Paltz, New York.